The
Beryllium
Eaters

By J. E. O'ROURKE

A NOVEL

Also by J. E. O'Rourke

Leaving Major Tela, a YA Novel

The Young Molly Maguires, a YA Novel

What's Your Story? -Essays on Worldwide Fiction and Writing Skills

Library of Congress Control Number: pending

ISBN-13: 978-0-578-73492-7

GAELWRITER PUBLISHERS

An imprint of J. E. O'Rourke

P.O. Box 335

Manchester, CA 95459

Table of Contents

CHAPTER 1—The Ore *1*

CHAPTER 2—Inca Myth *9*

CHAPTER 3—Kepo *19*

CHAPTER 4 – Eila *25*

CHAPTER 5—Drost *37*

CHAPTER 6—First Strike *47*

CHAPTER 7—The Cult *53*

CHAPTER 8—Holographs *63*

CHAPTER 9—Island Retreat *71*

CHAPTER 10—Slag Creation *83*

CHAPTER 11—Vasthi & Eila *93*

CHAPTER 12—The Macnessa *101*

CHAPTER 13—Mission Plan *113*

CHAPTER 14—Editing Slags *119*

CHAPTER 15—Tower Strike *127*

CHAPTER 16—Temple *137*

CHAPTER 17—Stadium *151*

CHAPTER 18—The Park *161*

CHAPTER 19—Apostates *171*

CHAPTER 20—Louke *179*

CHAPTER 21—Crustal Life *187*

CHAPTER 22—Taxila Ambush *197*

CHAPTER 23—Repository *207*

CHAPTER 24—Odyssey *219*

CHAPTER 25—The Crucible *231*

CHAPTER 26—Shooting Stars *237*

CHAPTER 27—Rancho Quecha *239*

CHAPTER 1—The Ore

The woman's bowler hat blew off in the wind as she bent to touch a crucifix to his head. He choked and convulsed on the sidewalk, arching his back in violent heaves. A surrounding knot of Indians in bright colored ponchos shrunk back.

"Move away from him, the man's having a fit."

A stout, gray-haired man huffed his way through the Indians and knelt, struggling to open the man's jaw using a wood splint to immobilize his tongue. He called to the Indians to help him hold the man, but they turned and hurried away into a gusting wind.

A short while later, Josiah sat at a sidewalk café with the doctor who had come to his aid. They switched to Spanish after finding Josiah was more fluent there than the doctor was in English.

"You are feeling well now, Senõr?"

"Yes, a little shaky, but better," Josiah said. "Thanks for your help."

A waiter came with their order: two beers, a dish of cut limes, and a plate of salt.

"I've never had this sort of thing happen until just a few months ago," Josiah said. "This was my third seizure. It's like I get a short warning bell, then everything short-circuits and I become a bit delusional." He squeezed lime juice onto the side of his hand, a pinch of salt, a taste, and tilted his head back as he drank from the bottle of beer. "Bother it all, I thought if you had this sort of thing it would show up when you were young—I'm almost fifty."

"Yes, it happens," the doctor said. He dabbed a lime wedge in the salt, took a bite of it, and drank his beer. "Is there something you suspect brought these seizures on, a period of illness, a traumatic event, something you can associate?"

"They began after I finally hit on a valuable mineral lode in these mountains."

"Ahh, you've found some gold, then?" He leaned over and gave a nudge to Josiah's shoulder.

Josiah paused, studying the doctor's age-lined face, the gray moustache, strong Indian features, and lively eyes. "Is doctor-patient confidentiality binding in Ecuador?"

"Absolutely," said the doctor, smiling.

"Beryl, a beryllium ore. There may be a few emeralds and aquamarine stones in it, but it's usually far more valuable for the beryllium metal content."

The doctor swept some coins from the tabletop into the hands of a pleading street urchin and shooed him away. "A metal worth more than emeralds?"

"They've discovered quite a few high-tech uses for it," Josiah said. "Nuclear plants, re-entry shields on spacecraft. They think it might prove valuable as a future solid fuel for powering spaceships." He finished his beer and ordered another round. "But I was hoping we could discuss more of

2

those delusional aspects of my seizures."

"Yes, tell me about the last episode, describe what you experienced."

Josiah drummed fingers on the table and began, hesitantly. "This time I was in the same place as in my earlier seizures—on a rocky, green-carpeted, mist-shrouded island, and a great, thundering sea nearby. A sweet smell of kelp hung in the air, and we stood around a bonfire listening to an old woman speak."

"We? What did the others look like—modern, ancient?"

"Ancient, perhaps Ireland, around the time of the Viking invasions there, everyone had that sort of battle gear, shields, swords, tunics. The old woman leaned on her tall shield and spoke to me."

"Were you armed, too?"

"No, I don't recall so. She seemed to think I was a Druid."

"Well, there's a puzzle. What do you know about Druids?"

"Not much, I think they held a sort of spiritual power among the Celts. Anyhow, she told me it was time to accept my calling to destroy an enemy."

"Did she describe who this enemy was?"

"She had a name for them. The Beryllium Eaters."

The doctor remained silent a few moments, watching Josiah from behind an impassive face. He abruptly straightened in his chair and the Spaniard in him surfaced in his lighted eyes and animated hands, "Yes, yes, I think I can see some connection between a perceived earlier existence and your mineral discovery that could have triggered this recall. Your discovery might have induced psychic phenomena that were the cause of your seizures. What you described conforms to some case histories I've come across. Leland Hinsie and others have reported in the literature that psychic attacks of certain individuals seem to represent a rapid and complete withdrawal from reality, and the assumption of an earlier existence."

"Am I losing my grip on reality?"

"Reality? Not even the great philosophers have understood the nature of reality. In the medical profession we study phenomenological observations. In any case, why should you stand for such an unpleasant mode of sending messages to you? If you will visit me in my office, we can do some examinations and I may be able to prescribe medication that will at least help suppress your seizures."

Josiah smiled at his pragmatic air. "Okay, I'll come and see you later."

He stayed talking with the doctor a while longer. They drank another round of beers and watched light fade from soaring, snow-capped peaks along the Avenue of the Volcanoes, north of Quito. When he rose to go, he took the doctor's card, promised to make an appointment, and hurried off to the Water & Power Agency.

"Ah, Ingeniero Josiah," Superintendent Hector said, and stood to shake hands across his desk. "You have had a good trip down from your work site?"

"Exhausting, but the results I got from the assay firm are exciting. The beryllium ore in the dike formation is even richer than I expected."

"Excellent, excellent," Hector said, rubbing his palms together. He opened a cigar box on his desk, invited Josiah to take one, and with shaking hands unwrapped a cigar for himself. Two fumbling cuts were needed to snip the cigar properly and he lit it from an ornate, heavy onyx lighter sitting on the desktop. He puffed for a few seconds; his eyes closed. "Magnificent," he murmured.

"Now all we have to deal with is an inconvenient situation," Josiah said. "Our little fortune is on a powerhouse site owned by the government."

Hector dismissed this with a wave of his cigar. He paced back and forth behind his desk, hands clasped behind his back, puffing, stopping to look out the window at the glorious, expansive view of the Andes. "How much metal will this ore yield?" he said.

Josiah drew up a chair and reached for a sheet of paper and pen from the desktop. "I'll sketch it out for you; our ore is in a wide dike intrusion that skews across the proposed powerhouse excavation, like this."

As he drew, Hector leaned to watch over his sketching. "Your dike enters and leaves our excavation plan so quickly," he said. "We'd only be able to recover a small amount of the ore in the planned excavation work." He straightened up and puffed clouds of smoke, thinking. "I could say our geologist, you, has studied the rock fracture directions and we need to turn the excavation to follow the same direction as the dike, no? Then we'll be able to mine more of this ore. What do you think?"

"The in situ rock pressures would actually be greater on the excavation walls in that direction, and these rock joints are weak in shear strength."

"Still, it could be done, no?"

"It would cost a lot more for things like rock reinforcement and thicker concrete."

"Ah, but the government can afford such things," Hector said. "We will turn the planned alignment to follow our ore body for the full length of the powerhouse. Your rock exploration report will show the wisdom of our new decision."

Josiah tapped his pencil on the desktop. It would cost a lot more. He sketched the new arrangement, made a few calculations, and whistled softly. "That should give us more than 100,000 tons of ore. With this high-grade beryllium content, we'll be rich. But now comes the big question. How are we going to move the stuff without anyone catching on— in some workers' lunch buckets?"

"I've already given thought to this problem. We were planning to construct a railroad spur from Larga, to transport electric generators that will be used in our powerhouse when excavation and concreting are completed. The railroad is not really needed for two more years, but we'll expedite building it anyhow and it will be ready early in the excavation phase."

Josiah leaned back and clasped his hands behind his head as he let clouds of puffed smoke drift upward. "So we'd use the railroad to haul away our excavated ore from the

6

waste rock piles. Okay, and what's our reason for moving waste rock off site and twenty miles across the mountains to Larga?"

Hector smiled and looked admiringly at his tasteful, expensive cigar. "You found the waste rock had some low-grade copper content. Not anything to get too excited about, but here's this completed railroad with nothing to do for at least another year. So, why not move the copper ore and sell it in Larga, to help offset our powerhouse costs? I might even award you an employee-of-the-year prize for your suggestion."

"And what do we do with the ore when it gets to Largo?"

Hector smiled. "The beryl ore will be off-loaded to stockpiles somewhere near Larga, until we have enough to contract with a metals firm willing to do a little discrete business with us."

"It sounds sort of workable, but it's got a lot of pieces to it. We might get tripped up at a half-dozen places before we finish."

"Leave it to me. Superintendent Hector goes unchallenged around here, and I have the useful political connections, if needed. We shall be rich men." Hector sat behind his desk, feet up on the top, and smiled. He broke into a raucous laugh and Josiah might have joined him, except now some things had changed. Eerie seizures and visions had entered his life and cast a new shadow on things

CHAPTER 2—Inca Myth

The old machine gave off a high-pitched whine as the driller eased his bit into the rock wall. He listened intently to the noise of the diamond-tipped bit eating into the rock and cupped a hand to catch drill water spilling from the collar of the hole. He rubbed the spill in his fingers, feeling for the quantity of fine rock cuttings in the water, and adjusted the drill machine's thrust on the bit. Josiah came up from the far end of the exploratory tunnel and stopped by the drill. He counted the number of remaining drill rods stacked beside it.

"I'm at the first sample depth," the driller said, anticipating his question.

The driller stopped his machine and shifted into pulling gear. The air motor lugged down as the machine strained, until the rock sample snapped loose from the intact rock deep in the hole. The driller and his helper finished pulling the steel rods from the hole and brought the rock sample out for inspection. Josiah took out a small magnifying glass carried on a thong about his neck and examined the sample. He sucked in a breath as he passed the glass over the pale blue crystals scattered in the rock. The beryllium content seemed even richer at this depth. He shoved the glass back inside his shirt.

"Take another sample two meters farther in," he said, and turned away to walk along the string of planks lying on the wet, muck-laden floor of the exploration tunnel. When the rusting steel ventilation duct projected too far out from the rock wall he stepped off the planks and slogged through sucking muck, too excited to keep from splashing mud on his trousers. He came out from the tunnel portal and sucked in breaths of soft, fresh air. The darkening sky promised rain soon. The roar of the river below drowned out the sound of his laughter. He'd even thought of singing, but spotted Julio, their new mechanic, kneeling beside a noisy, sputtering generator just outside the portal.

"What is it now?" Josiah said. "Is that machine going to last until we get the new parts?"

"The generator is very old, *Ingeniero*. I have not been provided with many tools, but I can manage. I wonder can you tell me when the excavation for our powerhouse will start?"

Josiah hesitated a few moments and sat on a boulder to look at the river below. "I'd like to know that, myself. The way things go around here it might depend on when the banana crop at Guayaquil ripens, or the date the turtles will return to the Galapagos Islands this year."

Julio grinned and sat on a boulder near him. "Yes, our country's remarkable Galapagos," he said. "You have read Darwin's journals?"

Josiah raised an eyebrow. "No, but I suppose evolution can go on, regardless."

"Indeed, yes it will," Julio said, almost whispering. "For the rocks on which we sit, for the turtles in the Galapagos, for you, for me, for all in this universe."

Josiah looked suspiciously at the erudite mechanic. It was difficult to make out the mechanics face in the shadow of his floppy, wide brimmed hat. "Tell me how this rock is going to evolve into something else," Josiah said.

10

Julio took on a somber face. "You are perhaps unaware of the geologist-philosopher de Chardin's belief that all matter in our universe has some level of consciousness?" He stooped to pick up a stone and turned it from side to side. "*Ingeniero*, this rock is a living, dynamic system of molecules, each with its own atoms and spinning electrons." Julio laughed at the incredulous look on Josiah's face. "*Ingeniero*, you and I are but a slightly more complex molecule than this rock, believe me." A sudden sputtering of the generator caught his attention and he leaped up to run to his machine. Throwing open the side panel, he pulled at the linkage within while adjusting a setting with his screwdriver.

"I wouldn't have thought you were such a knowledgeable dreamer," Josiah said. "What are they teaching in the trade schools these days—parapsychology or mechanics?"

Julio lifted his head above the cowl of the machine as Josiah got up to leave. "It is all one and the same, *Ingeniero*. I treat my machine as a fellow creature, and that is why it will keep running for me until our job is done."

"I don't care if you sacrifice your lunch to it," Josiah said, "but the day it pulls its last breath that's the day you'll be hoofing it down the road."

Julio leaned his elbow on the smoothly purring engine and laughed. He called after him, "Ah, *Ingeniero*, if you could only understand the half of what is in the world."

At the bottom of the slope, Josiah continued across the steel truss bridge. The water boiled and thundered beneath him as it rushed through a boulder-clogged strait. At the other end, he paused a few minutes at the foot of a long, steep trail leading up to the work camp. Rain drizzled down, and he shook out his folded parka, threw it over his shoulders and started up the trail.

The going was difficult. A heavier rain earlier in the day had mired the trail into a thick goop of mud and stones. Pack donkeys carrying heavy supplies for the exploration work had ruined the hand-placed stone cobbles and tree branches that had surfaced the trail. He rested at a switchback halfway up the slope.

Looking back across the river valley, dense, broad-leafed foliage covered the slope of the mountain. Higher up, soaring peaks jutted into vaporous clouds swirling past. He looked along the ridgeline to the north, stopping to gaze at the long, flat ledge, just before the mountain plunged steeply to a looping bend ahead in the river.

The scattered stones of Tupa Inca lay up there. He'd read the site had been the northernmost fortress of the great Inca ruler of that name. It commanded a view north along the river pass and guarded the Inca interior against any invasions from that direction. The ledge faded to a shadowy outline through the increasing drizzle.

When Josiah reached the work camp at the top of the trail his trousers below the poncho were soaked, and his inner shirt was damp with perspiration. One of the kitchen workers hurried to meet him with a glass of orange juice. Josiah emptied it in a single, long draught. He watched bleary-eyed at tunnel laborers playing soccer in the drizzle. They were mostly from small villages in the south. Only isolated Indian farmers lived in the mountains here and farther north.

He watched the game for a few minutes and walked inside the main building. The strong smell of diesel oil flared his nostrils as he walked back to the living quarters. The houseboy was finishing his weekly oil mopping of floors to combat the insects. Inside his quarters, Josiah shed his wet clothes in the small bathroom and tested the shower for hot water. The boiler had been turned on for the evening and so he showered and changed into dry clothes.

His drilling crew, some tunnel workers, and several engineers were in the camp's mess when he entered. Josiah took a seat next to the driller and the mess attendant served them bowls of soup.

"Good evening, *Ingeniero*," the driller said. "Before we quit today, we finished the drill hole. Will there be more work tomorrow?"

"Yes, but tomorrow should do it," Josiah said. "The next drilling after that will be for blasting. The main excavation begins in a week or two."

The hall grew quiet and the click of spoons and rattle of plates during the meal accentuated the lack of conversation and banter this evening. Something hung in the air. After eating, most of the men went immediately to their rooms. Only a few remained and drank coffee. Josiah spoke to an engineer at their table who'd been doing the survey of Hector's railroad spur from Larga.

"Any explanation for the disappearance of another of your railroad workers this week?" Josiah asked.

"The men will not speak to us about it," the engineer said. "But I heard whispers in the café at Larga." He hesitated, his cup poised in mid-air.

"What do they say?"

"This man and the other before him were taken by the fire-tongues."

A look of fright crossed the face of a mess attendant wiping their table. He stopped his work and hurried back to the kitchen.

"What's behind that story?" Josiah said.

"I suppose it's some sort of Indian superstition. This region is very isolated from the outside world and one hears strange stories here."

Josiah turned to his driller. "You were born and raised in these mountains. What do you know of fire-tongues?"

The driller rubbed at gray-stubble whiskers in his heavily creased cheeks. He squinted at the spoon he turned over in his hand, as if deciding what to tell the outsiders. "The fire-tongues are very real, *Ingeniero*." His voice was a raspy whisper. "They are gods who came here with the Inca and helped them in battle. It is said that the Inca sacrificed prisoners to them. Now that Inca warriors are no more, the fire-tongues are said to seek their own sacrifices."

The giant blades of the overhead fan pushed short, pulsing waves of warm air over them. Men lowered their coffee cups at an adjacent table and stared.

"Tell me more about them," Josiah said.

The driller shook his head. "If you wish to know more about the gods, it would be better for you to ask the old farmer, Kepo, who lives above our work camp. I am fearful of saying more, and perhaps angering them. I have a family, *Ingeniero*."

14

Julio watched from another table, coffee in hand, and Josiah turned to him. "They say you were born here, too. What do you know about this legend?"

"It is only a superstition," he said, "fed by stories of old men like Kepo, who mix our oral history with hallucinations brought on by the coca leaf. Learned men have seen strange gods in murals and metalwork left by the Inca, but I have not read anything of fire-tongues."

Josiah stared at him a few moments and turned away. No one pursued the matter any further. A few minutes later Josiah excused himself, rose, and went to his room. Inside, he studied the calendar tacked on a wall and went over to a desk near a window. He sat and looked out at the darkening line of mountain peaks. He found his starting point and traced that familiar profile to the long, flat ledge of Tupa Inca. It was almost lost now in the darkness. He combed his fingers through his hair and rubbed at his jaw. It wasn't only the discovery of the ore and the excitement of gaining sudden, illicit wealth that buzzed in his mind. Something else was going on, something frightening. Some dark thread connected the 'beryllium eaters' of his seizures, the ore, Tupa Inca, and the fire-tongues.

He got up and went over to his wardrobe shelf and took down a bottle of scotch and a glass, poured a few inches, and added a dash of water from a thermos on the desk. As he brought the glass to his lips he felt the aura take hold. Frightened, he set the glass down and clenched the edge of the desk. He trembled, squeezed his eyes shut, and groaned as the convulsions wracked his body. He fell to the floor and writhed as his mind clouded over.

In the dream that possessed him, the old warrior woman

spoke as before.

"We've summoned you again to order you to make haste with destroying the beryllium eaters."

This time he questioned her. "But who are these beryllium eaters and where do I find them?"

She laughed and took her sword to trace a line in the wet sand of the beach—three jagged peaks, continued on into a short, horizontal line, and ending with a sharp stroke downward—the profile of Tupa Inca.

"You'll find them on the mountain you've seen that lifts its spine to the heavens, like this. They are called fire-tongues by the Indians of that place."

"Where've the fire-tongues come from?" Josiah said.

She slashed the sand above the ridgeline, five lines to form a pentagon, and stabbed her sword into the center. "From another world," she said, her voice fading, "through this constellation of stars."

Josiah felt himself spinning and falling through an interminable blackness. He awoke lying on the floor of his room, tasting blood in his mouth. Rising in short, aching movements, he rubbed the stiffness from his arms and shoulders and stood at the window. A thin crescent moon and blankets of stars shone above the ridgeline at Tupa Inca. The memory of the warrior woman's tracing flooded over him and he searched the constellations. He found the pentagon of Puppis, almost lost among the fiery pinpoints of light around it.

It was only an aberration of his mind, he thought, myths

16

and knowledge that he'd stored up from reading, and which flooded over him now during his sickness. A fortune awaited him in that mountain, and a phantasmagoria with Celtic trappings weren't going to push his mind over the edge. A retirement of wealth and security was in reach and he'd be a fool to let such a weakness distract him. He paced the room, stopping every few passes to stare out the window at the stars. Beads of sweat formed on his forehead and he stepped into the bathroom to splash his face with cool water and rinse his mouth. The returning aura signaled another seizure coming on—the capsules, they were worth a try. His face dripping with water, Josiah pulled open the medicine cabinet. Shaving cream and razor toppled into the sink as he grabbed for the vial of capsules given to him by the doctor. He swallowed one with a glass of water and waited. A spasm shook him and he tried to cry out but no sound came. In seconds, the most painful convulsions he'd ever felt gripped him. The old woman's wild, shrieking laughter echoed back and forth in the blackness. Josiah thrashed around on the floor and beat his head against wall and tub. After the seizure passed, he lay frightened and gasping; saliva and blood trickled from the corner of his mouth. He became aware of a pounding on his door.

"*Senõr* Josiah, you are all right?"

"Yes, I'm all right. I just had a nightmare."

"I can get you something, a drink?"

"No, thanks, I'll be fine." He got up and went into the other room. Taking the vial of capsules from his pocket he dropped them into the wastebasket. The damned seizures were going to kill him. He dropped onto a chair by the desk and wiped blood from his mouth on a tissue. Something real

17

was happening, all those connections—the ore discovery, the seizures, the messages leading back to the ore. Now the fire-tongues—he'd lose his mind if things kept on. Maybe he could make a real effort to find out more about what the old woman was on about.

CHAPTER 3—Kepo

Over a few merciful weeks without seizures, the changes from daylight to dusk to dark had become imperceptible. Heavy rain clouds closed out any sunlight by early afternoon. The pillowing hulks gradually merged into a dense gray expanse that deepened to blackness as evening fell.

On an afternoon when the weather broke and the wind swept the last clouds from the sky, Josiah climbed the mountain to reach Kepo's house. The path wound back and forth in a series of switchbacks on the face of the mountain. Runoff water gurgled down channels eroded across the pathway making walking difficult. He stopped and rested often. A shepherd girl tending two cows and dressed in a bowler hat and knotted serape over her shoulders stood alongside the pathway. He stopped and tried to get her to speak, but she stood silently with staff in hand and watched him. Reaching into a pocket in his rucksack he took out an orange and gave it to her. She rewarded him with a bright smile, and he waved and went on. At more than one thousand feet above the river, he reached the narrow, terraced ledge on which Kepo's house stood. The old man went inside carrying a pail just as Josiah came into view. The light had faded from the sky and Josiah was winded and sweaty from the long, steady climb. Walking across the ledge to a low, stone-lined cistern, he shrugged off his rucksack and sat down. The cistern lay beneath a cleft in a rock outcropping, and a steel pipe jutted out to spill a slow, steady trickle of water. Using his hands, he caught some water and drank. He sat for a long time, watching the house and the darkening range of mountains.

"Kepo," he called. No answer or sound of movement came from the house. A wind rose and a few early stars pricked the dusky evening. "Kepo?" He picked up his rucksack and walked across the yard to knock at the door.

"Yes, yes, come in *Senõr* Josiah, come in," called a voice from the house.

Inside, a roughly made table and chairs stood next to a window looking out from the mountainside. A metal tub sat on a low bench in the far corner, and adjacent to it, a kerosene stove and a few dishes lay on top of an open-shelved cabinet. A pot of water boiled on the stove.

"Come in and sit, I will bring some light into the room." He took a kerosene lantern from the cabinet and placed it on the countertop.

"You know me?" Josiah asked as he sat at the table.

Kepo finished lighting the lantern and poured hot water from the pot into two cups. He brought the cups, a silver flask, sugar and spoons to the table.

"I guessed it was you. My nephew works in your tunnels in the mountain," Kepo said. "Please, have some coffee."

Josiah poured some of the thick coffee extract from the flask into his cup of hot water and spooned in sugar. The old man fixed a cup too, and they drank quietly for a few minutes.

"It grows dark; you will stay here tonight, of course," Kepo said.

"Thanks, I've brought a sleeping bag with me." He waited

for what felt like a polite interval and said, "I've come to learn about the fire-tongues from you."

Kepo flinched and set his cup down. "How did you know of them and why is it you are asking me?"

"We've had laborers disappear without a trace from our work camp. Our drill operator, a man who grew up around here, thinks it had something to do with what he called fire-tongues. He seemed too frightened to say more but said you might tell me about them." Kepo's eyes came alive in the lamplight but his face did not betray any emotion. "If these fire-tongues are attacking our workers I need to put an end to it," Josiah said.

"It could be dangerous for me to speak of these beings to you," Kepo said. "But I am an old man, the last of a noble Inca family, and I am not so afraid of them. My ancestors were among the Inca leaders permitted to enter the temple of the fire-tongues, to receive the magic talismans our warriors carried into battle, and to deliver enemy captives to be sacrificed after a victory."

"The fire-tongues are some sort of gods, then?" Josiah said.

"Yes, gods, who came from out of the sun and appeared to us on the great high plains in this country. At the time they appeared we were a little-known people of farmers and herders in the Andes. Our warriors were fearsome but were hard-pressed by our enemies. After we were chosen by the gods to be their people, no one could withstand us, and we built an empire such as never before seen."

"You sacrificed to them—how was that done?"

Kepo worked his withered mouth as if chewing the words. "It was told that the gods embraced their victims and flayed them in a fiery kiss of death. It was why they were called fire-tongues." He reached over and tapped Josiah's arm. "In the sacrifice of ordinary warriors, the man shook in the embrace of the god until he exploded into flames, and dusted the floor with a black soot. A sacrifice of the most noble and bravest of the enemy was different, and they received a special honor from the god. Such a person the god consumed slowly, bathed in a flickering glow of blue light. *Senõr*, the mortal image of the honored one could be seen to pass over onto the god before the soul drifted to the floor in ashes."

Josiah clasped his hands on the table and leaned toward Kepo. "The god came to look just like the person he fire-tongued?"

"Yes," Kepo said, spreading his hands outward and speaking in a hushed tone, his face and eyes emphasizing the mystery of his words. "And the gods in their new, mortal skins walked among our people and the conquered ones for up to three passages of the moon. Afterward, the images of those persons left the earth and the gods returned to the temple to await new battles and sacrifices."

They sat in silence for some minutes. The soft patter of rain brushed in waves over the house and dripped steadily in puddles beneath the roof eaves. Josiah combed a hand through his hair and sat back in the creaking, wood chair.

"If the fire-tongues are still around, where can they be found?" he said.

Kepo pointed higher. "On the ridge above us, at Tupa Inca," he said.

"Have you gone there to see them?"

"Oh no, Senor. Only a few Inca families who still serve the gods are permitted to go up there."

"I'll go tomorrow," Josiah said.

"Why?"

Josiah lifted a hand from the table, and let it fall. "A very old warrior woman told me in a dream that I had to find them."

Kepo chewed and nodded, seeming to accept this.

"How many fire-tongues are here?" Josiah said.

"Two are left, a male god, and a female goddess."

"What kind of appearance do they have, without a human's skin?"

"Their form is like ours, but the ancients used poetry to describe what they saw. They spoke of eyes that shone with the brilliance of the sun, and a woman who wore the colors of icy mountains in morning light."

Josiah twisted his mouth as he tried to imagine the creatures. "Are they of great strength? Can they die?"

Kepo was silent for a few moments. "Some stories spoke of a third god, a male fire-tongue who was destroyed, but it was not told how this could have happened," he said. "A fire-tongue in battle could run unscathed through clouds of spears and arrows and lay waste to hundreds of warriors armed with war clubs. No, I think it might not be possible to destroy a fire-tongue."

CHAPTER 4 – Eila

By midmorning Josiah had his crew started on the final drill holes. Afterward, he came out of the tunnel portal and started up the hillside.

Julio called to him, "*Ingeniero*, where are you going this fine morning?

"To collect rock samples. I'd be especially interested in conscious samples."

"Yes, yes," Julio said, breaking into a smile. "For certain, the more advanced specimens will be difficult to recognize. *Ingeniero*, you must excuse me if I ask now of other matters we might profitably discuss at your convenience?"

Josiah was startled. He turned on the pathway to look back. Had this conscious rock expert somehow found out about his discovery of beryllium ore? He decided he might need to fire Julio the first chance he got.

"Go back to your generator and keep an eye on it so we don't burn out that drill," Josiah said. "What do you think we're paying you for—to do interviews?"

"Of course, *Ingeniero*," he said, and plodded back toward the sputtering generator.

Josiah went on, climbing the trail slowly and pausing to rest at times.

It became warm and humid as the morning sun rose and moisture steamed from the foliage. He took out field glasses and scanned the work camp on the far mountainside. Labor crews were busy with the erection of posts and beams for the new dormitory building being prepared for a larger construction crew. Freshly gouged cuts along the flank of the mountain showed the progress of railroad construction. One crew constructed the railroad grade from the camp toward the railhead at Larga. Another crew worked to bring the grade down through a series of switchbacks, to a point just across the river from the powerhouse tunnels. He returned the field glasses to his pack. The railroad was almost done; Hector had moved quickly.

He resumed his climb above the powerhouse, and a couple of hours later walked across a flat, saddle area and turned north, along a ridgeline descending toward the ancient outpost of Tupa Inca. The bare, wind-swept ridge changed gradually to a broken terrain, and continued to drop through scattered small trees and clumps of brush. The foliage made it difficult to keep a straight bearing, but soon the ridgeline flattened, and the brush grew more stunted. With perhaps a kilometer left to go, he noticed a heavily timbered crib, jutting out from a broken expanse of rock on the west side of the ridgeline. An old mine entrance he decided and edged down toward it. Unhooking a geology pick from his belt, he sampled the rock around the portal. It had to be a surface projection of the beryllium ore dike that cut across the powerhouse deeper in the mountain. Except here at the surface it showed only slight traces of any beryllium content. He took a flashlight from his rucksack and went inside the mine. A short distance in, the rock became fresher and more competent, and the miners had discontinued their timber lining. Deeper in, the main tunnel was intersected by a number of smaller tunnels. He sampled a few spots with his pick. A quick examination with a pocket glass showed only weak traces of beryllium content. Hardly worth commercial mining, but they'd continued mining deeper. He went on, edging ahead and playing the beam of the flashlight on the surrounding walls. Suddenly, a figure stepped out from one of the side tunnels ahead. Josiah stopped and caught his breath.

"Lower your light."

Josiah lowered his beam. The face ahead was a black shadow beneath the miner's hat and lamp, and the miner wore muddy jeans and a baggy, open rain slicker.

"Who are you?" Josiah said, "and what are you doing here? This mountain is government property."

The laugh was throaty, and feminine. "Oh? But one thing at a time, Josiah. Yes, I know you. I am Eila, one of those you know as fire-tongues." Josiah went rigid with fear. "We've become interested in you since learning you were in charge of the excavation below," she said.

He backed away a step and tried to keep any sign of fear or worry in his voice. "Interested—why?"

Eila gestured with a sweep of her hand, "This mine has barely served our immediate needs for hundreds of years, but our project needs are much greater. Your new excavation below should be able to satisfy our project requirements."

She advanced a step and Josiah retreated one. "What requirements are you talking about?" he said.

"An increase in the amount of beryllium we seek," she said. Josiah caught his breath. "We've visited the exploration tunnels you've driven in your new powerhouse area," she went on, "and saw how you've encountered the same rock dike as up here. Your location seems hugely richer in beryllium content."

Josiah's hands shook—they were after his beryllium. "What's that to me, or to you? It's government property," he said.

"Is it? But with your help we might find a way to divert the ore from your project to our own."

"Why would I be interested in doing that?"

Eila laughed. "We know you've taken samples to be assayed and have reported regularly to the construction superintendent in Quito, but no one at the worksite seems to be aware of your discovery. It occurred to us that you might be planning to sell it for your own profit."

"And you'd like to receive a share of the money?"

"The beryllium itself is something far dearer to us." She came forward and Josiah felt rooted to the ground. She stopped a few feet from him, and her eyes glowed in the dark, shadowy outline of her face.

"I have come from the planet of Aquama, in a galaxy outside your own," she said. "We are the Skatha. Shall I tell you our story, Josiah?"

Sweat rolled from his brow. He needed time to assess what kind of danger she represented. "I'm listening," he said.

"Good, your life may depend on it. If you listen carefully the importance of your beryllium find will become apparent. Once, Josiah, our race was remarkably like yours. Our

28

planet received its energy supply in the form of electromagnetic emissions from twin stars in our galaxy. An imbalance between the positions of the stars occurred, and the energy plasma radiated by them plunged. Our planet began to fail. Plant life died and animals disappeared. We rushed to enable biochemical substitutes for organic life, but soon our own existence was in peril. The atmosphere cooled and new levels of what were now radioactive emissions erupted from the twin stars. Our scientists searched desperately for some way to shield us and provide radioactive protection to our organic being. Beryllium, a rare metal on both your planet and ours, offered a solution. We had long used it as fuel in thermal engines for space travel, and it became our salvation."

"You used it to construct some sort of space suit?"

"Our space suit is part of us; we were encapsulated within a beryllium sheath."

She placed a hand on his shoulder, but he withdrew from her touch. Eila laughed in her strange, chime-like manner. "Don't be alarmed, Josiah, I only meant to reassure you.

"You want to take the beryllium back to your own planet?"

"You're rather perceptive for your kind; yes, that was our original mission. However, Drost, the expedition leader, has another plan in mind. He's not aware that I don't share his ambitions, so what I'm telling you must be held in confidence. I fear his retaliation if he knew I would betray him."

"What's Drost's plan?" Josiah said.

"Ah, all in good time. Have I put you at ease about the sort

29

of beings we are?"

"Hardly. How close to being human are you?"

"Very close. I shall tell you a little about the creatures that we have become. When our catastrophe struck, our life scientists were infinitely more advanced than your own. They thought to take advantage of beryllium's reaction with oxygen to produce our body's heat energy and used its imperviousness to radioactivity to shield us. She broke into more of her strange laughter. "You don't see the brilliance of it—you are repulsed. Don't you realize that all your own immortal higher senses are grafted within an exposed, corruptible carriage of flesh and bone? Josiah, we discovered how to seal our organic being, all our higher senses, and the biological code of our race within a timeless beryllium engine."

The roots of his hair prickled, and his mouth grew dry as he watched Eila spin, arms uplifted, laughing wildly. She came suddenly to him and grasped his shoulders. Her laugh stopped abruptly as she looked at him, close enough now in the backwash of light for Josiah to observe her face. Beautiful humanoid features, exquisitely chiseled in gemstone coloring, green-hued, blue highlighted, thousands of facets of flashing points of light as she tilted her head.

"The experiment was not, however, all that we had hoped for," she said. "Almost our entire being was successfully encapsulated within a beryllium sheath. However, we were left bereft of the delicate mantle of sensory perception that you wear so well over your own body, Josiah, a tactile skin."

"Whatever you're showing looks quite spectacular. I had thought pure beryllium was a dull, gray metal."

30

"Our scientists were able to infuse some of the rare gemstone impurities of natural beryl into the metal sheath, for beauty's sake, to meet the desires of our women. However, in the initial experiments they had tried to provide the beryllium sheath with an almost infinite number of sensory receptors to simulate a natural skin. However, that proved to be an unbelievably difficult challenge. You cannot imagine what a work of organic art a human skin sheath comprises, and so they were ultimately unsuccessful. A disappointment, but they had to accept that a condition of living without a true skin mantle might have to be tolerated for some indefinite future while experiments continue."

Josiah was alert to the nuances in her voice. "Indefinite future?"

"Can you imagine what it is like to lose all the sensory perceptions of skin, Josiah? What I see in your eyes pains me. I am not so much different from you, but you look at me as if seeing only a robot endowed with intelligence. I wish I could have worn a skin sheath for our meeting. It would have been a beautiful thing to touch your face and feel the quickening of emotion, something that could not be compared with the electromagnetic sense perception that I must use. Can you fathom the magnitude of our loss, a human sheath that allows the inner being to commune with the world and with others of its kind?"

Kepo's story came crashing in on Josiah. "The fire-tongue ritual, and the wearing of a victim's skin for three months—that's what the Inca story is all about," he said.

The glow from Eila's eyes rose and faded. "Yes, it evolved from experiments Drost made after we first arrived here so long ago. We can now translate a human's organic sheath

31

onto ourselves. The organic, molecular composition of the human sheath is dissolved, ionized, and bonded onto our beryllium surface. Capillary passages in our beryllium structure enable sensory communication between our inner organs and our new organic sheath—for a few months, anyhow. It's an extraordinary if sinful accomplishment by Drost, however temporary the results may be before the skin deteriorates." She laid her hands on his shoulders and Josiah flinched. "Don't be alarmed, Josiah. You'll notice we're still talking peacefully, and for your further peace of mind, I've never made use of the fire-tongue ability."

"The stories the Indians tell me say that the Skatha have been here since the time of the Inca Empire. That's about sixteenth century I'd guess; just how long do you Skatha live?

"Our normal life span on Aquama before the cataclysm was about 200 years. With the advances our scientists made during their beryllium sheathing research and the nature of our—and your—cell growth and decay mechanisms, they've been able to extend that life span with a sheath to perhaps 700 to 800 years. We have something like the electronic pacemaker for your heart disorders beneath our beryllium sheath. Ours regulates our organic cell chemistry, prolonging the growth and prime cycles and suppresses the onset of the dying cycle for our biologic cells. I would suppose you and I are near the same middle-age stages of our lives.

"Awesome. Am I to meet Drost, too?"

"Not until I've prepared you; he's a danger to you, and if he acquires control of an expanded beryllium source, many of your people will be in danger."

32

"Just by him fire-tonguing a handful every year?"

"Not too pleasant a thought if you're one of them; however, recently he has become consumed by thoughts of achieving absolute mastery over large populations, something like we had during the Inca empire. He's been experimenting over the past several years and has resolved some remaining technological problems for achieving this mastery. He's found an internal process for using the science of bio-metallurgy to greatly expand an ordinary human subject's intellectual power."

"Maybe he's not too aware of the huge firepower of nations outside this small country."

"Once he enslaves a cadre of altered intellects to his own, absolute authority he expects to be able to overcome any obstacles. Come, walk outside with me and I will explain the rest."

He walked back to the portal with her, uncomfortable with the presence of her hand on his shoulder. Outside, the sun was low in the sky and a stiff breeze swept over the ridge.

"In Drost's studies, humans seem to have been willing, even eager, to submit their powers of intellect to all sorts of external authority, though such submittal has often been tentative and conditional. In Drost's plans, however, submission is designed to be absolute and irrevocable."

Josiah wondered if, in the end, he'd be permitted to walk away from this encounter. Why was she telling him all this? Perhaps he was to be forced into their experiments? He shuddered.

"How does he accomplish this transformation of a

person?" he said.

"By a process he calls slagging. The subject ingests a solution of computer programmed beryllium oxide nano-strands mixed in an organic catalyst. Programming includes the political precepts of Machiavelli and the philosophy of Nietzsche, to name but two of your intellectual models that Drost has selected. The programming is designed to ensure Drost's slags will rise to positions of extraordinary power in your world affairs. After being given the solution, the initiate is fire-tongued, but at a very low energy level. It is not enough to cause a skin transfer but can internally synthesize Drost's programed strands into a slag's biological being."

Josiah lifted her hand from his shoulder. It was curiously light for what he'd imagined for a metal-clad limb. "Where do you stand in all this?" he said. "Aren't you in on his plans?"

"I would like only to gain control over as large a supply of beryllium as possible. I would need some of it for refueling our craft, to enable a return to my own planet, my own people. The rest would be given to our scientists to help satisfy our chronic need for the metal. It was one of the reasons we and other spaceships were sent into space so many years ago. Drost, however, has perverted this mission."

Dark clouds had appeared above the jagged horizon and enveloped the fading sun. The breeze stiffened and Eila removed her miner's hat. Her long, silvery hair floated and whipped in the coursing wind, and her face coloring became a darkening aquamarine in the dimming light. The wind blew open her rain slicker and flattened a cotton shirt and trousers against a very human-like form. He had to stare—not bad for reconstructive metal sculpting. Eila watched him, and

34

obviously amused.

"Perhaps you could perceive me as attractive?" she said. "You might even wonder how similar to your own women I might actually be? Our manner of making love is quite the same, for example." Though unable to generate clear modes of facial expression, she was artful in creating mood with the musical range of tone in her voice.

"That's a bit hard to imagine, but I needn't pursue it," he said, combing his fingers through his hair. "Where's your spacecraft now?"

"The spacecraft? Oh yes, our spacecraft. Come, I'll take you now to Tupa Inca."

"I thought you said I'd be in danger from Drost?"

"Trust me," she said. "He's waited for me to make contact with you for many days already. You must meet him and agree to whatever he demands. We shall work together afterward to alter his plans."

He wondered if he could trust her, but he had to go. At least until he could cash in with Hector and escape this nightmare.

CHAPTER 5—Drost

It was an hour hike to the brow of Tupa Inca. Stunted, wind-swept brush threaded across a field of tumbled and scattered stone blocks. Two level platforms of fitted blocks were barely visible above the encroaching brush. Eila led Josiah to one of the platforms and onto a smooth, dark-surfaced stone. She took a transmitter from her pocket and seconds later the stone descended into the ground.

They passed a landing platform as they went down. "That leads to the holding bay for our spaceship, the Epoch-3," she said. "It hasn't been used since we had the Indians carry it up here, piece-by-piece, from where we first landed in Peru. We've removed a small reconnaissance craft from it, called a Griffin, and stationed it on a separate lift to the surface. We use the Griffin occasionally, but sparingly, since it, too, is powered by beryllium, and it has been necessary to ration our scarce resources of the metal."

The stone block halted its descent and a door flashed open in a wall of the shaft. Eila led the way along a passage carved through rock and lighted by long panels of blue lights, inset to the walls near the top. The polished stone panels along the way had been carved with scenes of Inca battles, and were separated by borders of hammered gold sheets. She halted in front of a long, transparent, plastic panel set into a wall of the passageway.

"Inside is Drost's bio-metallurgy laboratory," she said.

Skeins of glinting, ultra-fine metallic threads spooled beneath a machine next to a large computer screen. The screen scrolled through sets of mathematical data, schematic diagrams, sets of multilingual tables, and logic diagrams. All appeared and disappeared at blurring speed on the computer screen as the threads spooled.

"You're watching the programming of beryllium strands," she said. "They're later fragmented to molecular size and added to the slagging solution. A single dose impregnates a human blood stream with billions of nano-size beryllium oxide memory strands, with a combined storage capacity greater than might be found at an astrophysics laboratory. Selected average human beings will acquire a programmed wisdom probably exceeding the combined knowledge of all your Nobel Prize winners."

"Was all that apparatus developed after you came here?" Josiah asked.

"No, most of our more sophisticated equipment was brought with us on the Epoch-3. Come, I'll show you our decidedly cruder metallurgy plant."

She turned off the central passageway, through a doorway, and led the way onto a narrow metal grating overlooking a deep, open pit area. A glowing furnace took up the near end of the pit, followed by a long, rotating mill, another furnace, a final array of vats, helical metal coils, molds, and at the far end, a power station. A few Indian workers were seen scattered throughout the facilities.

"Shall I describe the preparation of pure beryllium from the ore?" she said.

"I think I've had enough, for now," he said, overwhelmed by the scale of the enterprise.

"Such enthusiasm," she chided. "In any case Drost has now decided to accelerate his program if he can obtain additional beryllium. Our plant has been able to process enough beryllium for our personal maintenance needs and to build up a small stockpile for our original mission, but it's inadequate to also carry out his new slagging program."

"Personal maintenance needs—what does that mean?"

"We must consume several grams a day, to replace that used by our thermal oxidation effects."

"You mean you eat the stuff?"

Eila laughed. "We eat organic food for our inner body— 'for the athlete inside you'—as your cereal boxes say. However, the beryllium supplement is metabolized onto our sheath in an electrolytic process to resupply an amount lost in daily oxidation effects. Maybe it's not so different from you taking iron in a vitamin supplement?"

Josiah grimaced, "Yes, right, we're so alike, aren't we? How did you manage to get all this equipment built down here?"

"We've always had an ample supply of Indian laborers and artisans, families chosen and pressed into hereditary service to us long ago by the Incas. Shall we continue on?"

They left the metallurgy plant and walked to the end of the stone passageway, through a bronzed doorway, and into a lavishly appointed apartment. High above on a polished, black stone ceiling, sparkling gemstones were inset in patterns that Josiah gradually recognized as the star constellations—Orion, Lepus, Eridanus, and, chillingly, the pentagon, Puppis. A thin, high-intensity light beam radiated from a dazzling emerald set within Puppis. Eila watched him as he stared at the brilliant emerald.

"What's the significance of the lighted gemstone inside Puppis?" he said.

"That represents our planet Aquama. It does not actually lie within Puppis, which is in your own galaxy. Puppis is a beacon pointing us toward our deeper galaxy."

"I'd have to guess Aquama would be thousands of light years distant. How is it possible you could have reached here, and expect to return, in any conceivable length of time?"

Eila smiled and nodded. "You're amusingly alert, Josiah. However, our route from A to B in space travel is not a linearity measured in light years. Once the Epoch-3 reaches outer space, we can activate an onboard Quantum Generator, input coordinates of a galactic target, and the generator will develop an appropriate wormhole in space. Your own scientists are aware of wormholes in space but are lightyears behind us in harnessing them. Our passage through a wormhole to a distant galaxy is relatively swift. It takes longer to navigate Epoch-3 to our planet within our galaxy than it takes for the entire passage through a wormhole."

Eila led the way down an entrance hall and into a dimly lit, large room. Another vaulted ceiling soared overhead and pinpoint lights splashed across the black expanse. Josiah stopped and looked up at the tiny flickers of light. They didn't form any constellations he recognized. Farther ahead, at the rear of the room, a figure sat on a raised, semi-circular platform. Footlights spaced around the platform cast a cold, green lighting onto the seated figure. Eila escorted him to the platform, and Josiah stiffened as he looked up.

"Julio. You're the other Skatha."

Julio smiled, rose from his chair, and looked to Eila.

"I've had time to tell him something of our nature, and our plans," she said.

He returned his attention to Josiah. "Yes, Ingeniero, it's Julio, for just a while longer, but I am also the Skatha named Drost. I've worn the sheath of our master mechanic for almost three weeks now. An interesting man, your Julio." He held his hands in front of him and stared at them, then brushed them over his eyelids, nose, and mouth, speaking in a low, hushed tone. "Such a wondrous mantle of sensory delight. Even his coarse woman gives me pleasure I could not otherwise achieve with our own sophisticated but uninspiring sense preceptors. A human's organic sensors are often untruthful in what they perceive, but there is no substitute for the stimulation they provide our inner, organic being." He dropped his hands and sighed. "But the sheath is so terribly short-lived. Often, I am forced to go for months, sometimes even more than a year, without a human sheath. To prey too heavily on the Indians of these mountains is not without its dangers. Has Eila told you of our former comrade?" he said.

"Nothing yet of Crog," she said.

Drost smiled ruefully. "During a particular period many years ago, Crog and I lost control of our passion for experiencing the senses of men. We no sooner possessed the sheath of one, and without wearing it for even a tenth of its serviceable life, we were into another victim's sheath. It became almost impossible to sate our appetites. Then the Indians, normally terrified of us, banded together under one of their bravest shamans. A trap was laid for Crog at the farm of an intended victim. They captured him in a net of steel cables and buried him alive, still bound, at seven meters deep to be certain he'd stay put. I imagine he didn't last too much longer down there than an ordinary man."

"They didn't try to run you down, too?" Josiah said.

"No, they weren't brave enough to lay siege to Tupa Inc, and I was frightened enough by what they'd managed to do that I stayed ensconced here for years afterward."

Drost became agitated with the telling of this story and paced back and forth. "But that's all behind us. Soon, I shall never have to fear human retribution, regardless of my Skatha appetite for sensual pleasure. A powerful, new organization will be at my disposal, to do with as I wish."

Josiah looked to Eila, but she stared away.

"Eila has told you of my plans for slagging humans—Yes? Good. "The slags will have a commanding presence throughout your world. I will see that they are positioned in such key areas of power that I'll be able to give complete expression to all my needs and pleasures, and with total impunity." His dark eyes flared with an inner light. "They will be disposed to accept me as their god, and Eila as goddess. Kneel, Josiah, and pray for the sacramental drink that will ennoble you and bind you to my service." Drost's eyes set deep in a gray hued, sallow face took on a contorted, frightening visage.

"You're insane," Josiah said.

Drost tossed back his head and laughed. Eila laid her hand on Josiah's arm and whispered, "No, play along or you are lost."

Drost choked off his laughter and regarded the two of them.

"Look at her, *Ingeniero*," he said in a throaty murmur. "She has had this debilitating fascination for you since first laying eyes on you weeks ago. As for me, I believe I may now have had enough of your contentious nature. You might not fit my plans after all."

"Drost—we had a bargain," Eila said.

Drost smirked at Josiah. "I told her you needn't be slagged if we could persuade you to acquire the beryllium we need, but I sense a danger in you. I prefer to have greater control over you."

Josiah's fear rose in his throat. His chest tightened and he felt the waves of paroxysm mount in his brain, signaling the onset of a seizure.

Drost said to Eila, "Very well, my dear. Take this cup and have him drink from it, and then you may embrace him and flash our first slag into being. Or shall I?"

"No, don't do this," she said. "You promised you wouldn't."

Josiah let out a scream and fell writhing to the floor. Startled, Eila stepped away from him, looked at his spittle-flecked mouth and quivering form, and turned to Drost, "The electromagnetic emissions from him—what do you make of them?"

Drost raised his arm as if to shield his face. He crouched and stared at the thrashing form on the floor. "It can't be."

"It's in the waveform of the Galactic Druids," Eila said.

"That's impossible," Drost said. "This is just some sick, mortal being slithering across the floor. Look—he's grown still. Is the foul creature dead?"

Eila knelt beside Josiah. "He's breathing quietly, and his emissions are now faint, but still detectable." She continued to stare down at him. "I think he's recovering, but you can't slag him," she said. "Such aberrant emissions as he's shown could abort your programming of the memory strands."

"You could be right, but it may only cost us his sanity or life to try."

"Don't be a fool. You—we—need him to gain control of this new source of beryllium. Don't you see that?"

Drost scowled and glared at her. "Take the fool out of here and see whether you can bind him to our needs with your wily craft. Listen carefully; if you fail, there is no other alternative now except to attempt to slag him, whether he dies or not."

Eila cradled Josiah's head in her arms and wiped the trickles of blood from his mouth with her scarf. She placed her arms beneath his shoulders and knees and lifted him. Staring at Drost for a moment, she turned and carried Josiah away.

44

Josiah awoke later in the chill, night breeze sweeping over the surface of Tupa Inca. He lifted his head from Eila's lap and stared at the dim outline of a disk-shaped dome sitting atop one of the stone platforms.

"I've brought up the reconnaissance craft," Eila said.

He looked from her to the craft again. "Maybe it's all just one, long dream."

"Am I at least an attractive part of your dream?" she asked.

He studied her face. The moonlight washed over her, casting her delicate features now in shades of greens and amethyst and highlighting the silver of her hair. She seemed deceptively delicate in contrast to the strength he suspected she possessed.

"Yes, and probably the most extraordinary being I could imagine," he said, rising to a sitting position.

"That's a rather mechanical response. Could you love me?"

Josiah's face showed his uneasiness. "But we're too different," he said.

"No, not so different, Josiah, not so different," she whispered, and helped him to his feet. "Perhaps sometime soon I might prove this to you. But come, I'll take you back across the river. Drost has learned that you were to go to Quito tomorrow, to report on progress in removing the beryllium ore from the excavation."

Josiah rubbed at his jaw. "How did he know I was acting

with someone in Quito?"

"He followed you there on your last trip. He was pleased to learn that Superintendent Hector has now made arrangements to move the ore to Larga for processing. That eased many of our concerns, but Josiah, from this point onward, you must be completely open with me and keep me advised of all that happens. By helping me, you will be able to counter Drost, and save your world from a terrible threat."

"Suppose I'm able to help secure the beryllium for you to take back to Aquama; what do you propose to do about Drost? Would you help me if I had to destroy him?" he said.

Eila was silent for a few moments before she answered. "If you prove faithful to me, I won't fail you. You must ask no more than that for now."

He was unsteady on his feet and she took him by the arm to walk to the Griffin. Taking her transmitter from her jacket, she aimed it, and a panel lifted in the domed upper portion. She stepped up into the module and Josiah followed. Within seconds the Griffin hummed and emitted a fluorescent, bluish light from the tubular rim around the lower pod. The panel door hissed shut, the craft lifted from the pad, and soared out over the mountainside and across the river.

CHAPTER 6—First Strike

The excavation of the powerhouse rock from the beginning to where it finally crossed the ore dike had taken almost two months. Julio connected electric wires at blasting holes in the rock face and Josiah stood a short distance behind, watching the work. The other powder monkeys finished their wiring and they all began leaving the face.

"Relax *Ingeniero*," Julio said. "This will be the last round we pull and our beautiful beryl dike will have finished yielding its treasure."

Josiah gathered together some brightly colored blasting wires and weighed them down with a rock on the excavation floor. It had taken only the past three weeks to mine through the rich dike ore. So much time, and still he'd done nothing to destroy the beryllium eaters. Sweat beaded his forehead as he stared at Julio. This being was monstrous and evil, and there was no reason to hesitate in carrying out his assignment. But the other one. He wiped his forehead with a sleeve. How could he bring himself to destroy Eila? Would that be necessary, too? "Almost ready, Julio?" he called. It felt ghoulish, using the name attached to the skin sheath Drost wore.

Julio began a final check of the wiring. "Almost, I'll only be a few minutes longer." Josiah turned to leave. "One moment, *Ingeniero*. I'd like a few words with you while we have this chance to talk alone." Josiah stopped and turned. "By the end of this week the last of this beryl ore will have left for Larga. Have you informed Superintendent Hector you've found a buyer for the beryllium and that the ore should be processed quickly?"

"Yes," Josiah said, and he swallowed to wet his throat.

"Good, your price is outrageous, but I've assessed my gold storage at Tupa Inca and I can pay it. You will profit handsomely with your share, but it will be nothing compared to what I can deliver to you in the future. Continue to serve me, and when I've created my legions of slags reaching across every sea and into every continent, you will receive wealth and power in measures beyond anything you ever dreamed."

"There's a lot left standing between now and then," Josiah said.

"Everything is in motion," Julio said. "Beginning in your own country, you will soon hear of the birth of an organization I started this past year to serve as my recruiting arm for the preferred types to be slagged: students, intellectuals, scientists, politicians."

"It's going to take some time to make all the final arrangements and process the ore. Your slagging enterprise may have to be kept on hold for a bit."

Julio scowled. "No, we'll start immediately and shall use the small reserves of beryllium I've obtained from our surface mine. Take care that I do not find you and Hector lax at your duties. You are to complete our beryllium transaction in the shortest time possible."

"We'll do our best," Josiah said, and turned to hurry away

48

from the rock face. It took only a few minutes to walk back to a side tunnel where a worker knelt with the blast detonator. "All clear—shoot it," Josiah said, and he set his earplugs.

The man nodded and pushed on the plunger. The blast shockwave rolled back into the side tunnel, sending a thrum of shockwaves back and forth. Josiah glanced at his watch, took out his earplugs as he waited, and hurried back to the main chamber. He held a handkerchief to his nose and mouth and coughed from the acrid blast fumes as he stumbled ahead to the excavation face. The mucking crew wouldn't come forward for another twenty minutes and he wanted to be the first to discover the accident. At the face, his eyes watered as he searched the broken mounds of blasted rubble. No remains were in sight, whatever they might look like now. Perhaps Julio would be scooped up in the front-loader and disposed of in the muck pile without anyone even noticing his parts and pieces. It was kind of sardonic, thinking of Drost's beryllium sheath being melted down with the rest of the ore when it reached the smelter.

As Josiah stared, a mound of rock started heaving and sliding near the foot of the rubble pile. To his horror, a blackened figure rose out of the rock pile and staggered toward him. Tattered and torn shreds of Julio's skin clung to Drost's face and upper body. He grasped Josiah's arm and held him.

"You filthy worm—you thought to destroy me."

He pulled Josiah toward him, one hand behind Josiah's head, and struggled to bring his mouth onto Josiah's. The torn and shredded face, the putrid human mouth partly hanging from the beryllium skull—Josiah's heart pounded.

"Stop, Drost, it was a mistake," he shouted. Drost cocked his head. "Yes, yes, a mistake," Josiah said. "I'd called to the blaster to wait but he thought it was the signal to blast."

Drost hesitated, uncertain. Deep moans escaped his lips. His hand trembled as he patted the torn skin on his brow. The pain and confusion that reached into his organic brain brought a glazed, pinched look to his eyes. Up close, a glow seemed to emanate from behind the dark irises.

"Be sensible," Josiah said. "If you kill me you may lose your chance at the beryllium when the crew reports me killed. Hector may get frightened and abort our plans."

"I could wear your sheath and finish the deal acting as you," Drost said.

Drost tugged at a loose strip of his mouth. After a few moments he nodded and released Josiah, stepped back, and stood erect. His mouth opened with a glow and a flickering white aura surrounded his body. He brought both hands up and lifted his fingers to his opened mouth.

A piercing flash of blue light blinded Josiah for a few seconds. When he could see again, Drost stood before him with charred threads of clothing hanging from him and no sign of a skin covering remained on his beryllium form. He no longer moaned with pain.

"That which brings us great pleasure by its very nature must also be capable of bringing us great pain," Drost said. "Fortunately, our skin mantle can be shed as easily as it can be donned."

Josiah stared, hypnotized, at the dull, yellowish gray metallic finish of Drost's face. "Your beryllium sheath—it's so different from Eila's."

"The cosmetic practice of women adding mineral impurities of gemstones to glaze their metal sheath held no attraction for me," Drost said. "I will accept your explanation for the accident—this time. If something like this happens again, you will rue the mishap."

Drost walked behind a timber blast barricade and a few minutes later came out wearing a miner's hat and an oilskin poncho hanging to his feet. "You can report to the camp superintendent that your foreman Julio has resigned his post," he said. "I will keep in touch with you, *Ingeniero*. Your destiny is tied up with my own." He turned and walked toward the tunnel portal.

Josiah was still shaken from his close encounter when he felt the dream aura take hold again. He tried to remain calm and not struggle against falling into the abyss. He slid his back down against the wall and rolled to his side on the floor. Clouds of dust hung in the air, reflecting the ghastly glow of incandescent lights strung along the excavation roof. The swirling dust parted and the old warrior woman sat on a slab of rock, her sword held point-down on the rock floor.

"I tried and failed, but I haven't given up, old woman," he said.

"My name is Akla," she said. She twisted and worked a stiffness from her mouth. "We seem to summon poorly qualified Druids these days, Josiah. You need to take better care to credit the great strength and cunning of your adversary. You failed that time, but you must take heart and strike again, and soon, before he spreads his evil across this world."

Josiah hesitated, "I'll manage, but I don't want to destroy Eila. She's never taken part in the fire-tonguing of Indians and wants no part of Drost's plans for slagging humans. She wants only to return to her own world."

Akla leaned back, and her features shifted from amusement to a shrunken and wrinkled doubt. Finally, she laughed. "Knowledge of such evil without acting is also culpable, Druid. Eila may have felt powerless against Drost till now, but we shall see if she aids you against him. If she betrays you, she must be destroyed along with him. Be wary of her, lest you lose your immortal soul to the guile of this creature."

Clouds of dust coalesced, and the vision of the old woman was obscured. He shouted to her, "Wait, you need to tell me more about destroying Drost. Is what the Indians did to Crog the only way?" When he revived he was still shouting at clouds of dust hanging in the excavation.

CHAPTER 7—The Cult

Weeks later at the camp Josiah flipped through a tattered sports magazine, pausing now and then to look at the knot of men surrounding two chess players. Rain drummed on the corrugated tin roof accentuating the muggy silence of the recreation room. Wet rain slickers hung over empty chairs in corners and dripped puddles onto the oiled, timber floor. The camp manager flicked on a radio and leaned with elbows on the countertop, staring vacantly into the room. The ballad of the radio singer was too sad for the dreary weather and he switched stations. Static crackled till he found a newscast from Quito on one of the bandwidths that worked.

"—The Middle East situation continues to deteriorate daily. In North American news, a curious social phenomenon, curiously related to our own past in Peru, is taking shape in several large U.S. cities. A New Age environmental society, with mystical Inca trappings, seems to be winning large numbers of adherents—"

Josiah looked up from his magazine, listening to the newscast.

"Postulants are said to range from the aimless youth of the cities to dedicated leaders in science, government, and academic circles. The organization is known as the Inca Foundation, and we have tonight a taped interview with a young university student at one of the Foundation's temples in San Francisco—"

Several men turned from the game at the mention of 'Inca' and gave their attention to the broadcast. Josiah put aside his magazine and leaned on the arm of the chair as he listened. The throaty voice of a young woman attracted another couple of listeners away from the game.

"It's so important to relate to some sort of—of an awareness of our intimate relationship with the environment and our oneness with all of creation," she said, in her crooning voice. "This awareness is so very difficult to achieve, however, because of the estrangement of—of persons from their own commonality with all matter on our spaceship, Earth, whether from the rocks we ravage from Earth's mantle for our rampant mining needs, or from the mammals we slaughter for our food and hides industries—"

Josiah stood and went over to the countertop to hear her voice better over the drone of the rain.

"The Foundation offers us a way of healing this breach with our environment. By assigned studies and meditation, our members may proceed from the first level of Amoebic Darkness, to the ultimate level of Molecular Light, where we will have achieved a complete fusion of organic and inorganic awareness—"

The announcer interrupted with a string of commercials and men shook their heads and turned back to the chess game. Josiah went back to the reading table and picked up a news magazine. He scanned the index and found an article on the Inca Foundation. Reading quickly, he put it down and picked up another news magazine and found a similar article. The radio interview with the young woman resumed, continuing more of the heady language of environmental awareness and consciousness-raising, until the program ended. Josiah walked to the row of apparel hanging on the wall, took down his rain slicker, lifted a hardhat from a peg, and walked outside.

Hours later, the rain had eased before he reached the cabin. Kepo had seen him coming and waited by the door. He took Josiah's slicker and hardhat from him as he entered and gave him a long, woolen poncho. Josiah wrapped himself in it and stood near the woodstove. Kepo prepared a hot mug of coffee for each of them and they sat at the small table by the window. Josiah had barely begun questioning Kepo's memory on tales of how the fire-tongues might be vulnerable—whether from spears, or bullets, when Kepo suddenly stood and pointed out the window.

"*Ingeniero*—the jewel woman, she is coming."

Josiah leaned forward on the table and watched. The eerie blue glow loomed larger and larger until the Griffin hummed motionless above them. A change in pitch of the low-frequency hum, and the craft descended. They rose from their chairs and went to the doorway. The lights of the Griffin dimmed and went out. A pneumatic hiss, and a door panel in the craft slid open. Eila appeared dressed in a dark jumpsuit. Her face was masked in shadow, in contrast to the white, silvery sheen of her hair. She stepped lightly to the ground and approached Josiah.

"Josiah, it's good to see you again. Hello Kepo."

The old man stammered, blessed himself with the sign of the cross, and hurried back inside the house.

"How did you know I was here?" Josiah said.

"Drost observed you making the climb up the mountainside," she said, coming onto the porch. A long silence ensued as Eila watched him. "Interesting, the

55

feelings you elicit in me, Josiah. Quite unSkatha-like in their precocity—I don't recall ever sensing such things in the presence of a human."

"I'd greet you with a kiss, Eila, but I'm a little worried about keeping my skin. I don't think I'd look very good on you."

Eila's iridescent smile was perhaps mechanical, but the light, musical peals of her laughter held the warmth of her response. She turned to the Griffin, held out her command module to activate a button, and the Griffin rose vertically until it was out of sight.

"A precaution," she said, pocketing her module. "I've put it spinning in a holding position far above any ordinary air lanes."

Josiah extended his hand, and she stumbled against him as she came up onto the porch. His bravado fled as her face came within inches of his own. She placed her hand against the back of his shoulder and brought her mouth closer to his. Her lids shuttered half-closed and dimmed the brightness within. Josiah stood stiff as a post. She tilted her head back and watched him, then sighed and stepped away. Josiah took his first breath over the past minute.

"What would have happened if our lips had touched?" he said.

"Josiah," she said, exasperated, "if I were going to fire-tongue you, do you think I'd have bumbled about so?"

"I don't know. Why would you want to kiss a human without having in mind a fire-tongue episode?" She turned away and no one spoke for several moments. Josiah found his voice, "I brought some wine with me from the camp. Can

56

the Skatha drink alcoholic beverages?"

She hesitated and nodded. "We can and they can have the same effect on us as on you. After all, we have an inner physiology just like yours."

"Of course, I should have remembered what you told me. Let's go inside."

Kepo sat in the farthest corner of the room away from the doorway. "Please bring the wine and another chair for the table, Kepo, and join us." Josiah said. He beckoned Eila to sit at the table with him.

Kepo hurried to bring the wine, then excused himself to retreat back to his corner and would not be persuaded to drink with them.

Josiah turned his attention to Eila, "What's the purpose of your visit here?"

"I would have sought you out sooner simply to visit with you, but I was afraid it might lead to a nasty confrontation with Drost. I am not ready for that, not yet. He wants some news on when the beryllium processing will be completed and ready for delivery."

Josiah lifted his hands. "It took longer to set up the special facilities needed by the processing plant than we'd estimated. The processing is only now getting underway. But worse than that, the plant owner said it's going to cost more to process and he's demanded another hefty cost increase. Our price for delivering the beryllium to Drost will have to be doubled." Josiah decided this had already been far more unsettling than he'd ever imagined and deserved a further increase over and above his share of the profits with Hector.

Eila exhaled sharply. "Drost isn't going to like that. I don't know if he can meet such an increase with the amount of gold he has at Tupa Inca. Well, we shall have to see what happens when I report this."

Josiah shrugged, "We'll try to keep any more cost increases to a minimum." He took a long swallow from his wine glass and emptied it. "Tell me more about yourself," he said, as he refilled his glass and topped up hers.

"What do you want to know?"

Josiah looked out the window into the star-filled sky. The call across time to serve as a Galactic Druid bothered him slightly less now. Whether real or hallucinatory, he'd just have to get through it. It also helped his conscience to imagine his druidic role counterbalanced his larceny. "Do you believe in any sort of reincarnation?" he said.

"It was a belief of our race until the catastrophe happened on our planet, and our scientists offered this as perhaps our interim reincarnation," she raised her arms, hands spread, and dropped them. "Are we now nearer to being immortal, as long as our beryllium engine remains intact? I don't know, but I often wonder whether what we did was the best solution. Would it have been better to face extinction and look forward to the promised reincarnation? If that is a law of the universe, and many races in space believe so, might we have trusted nature to perpetuate us? At times, Josiah, I fear we may have defied a higher force and will be made to pay a terrible price."

Josiah opened the other bottle of wine and refilled her glass.

"Take caution," she said. "I have already drunk too much."

She watched, amused, as he stiffly poured his own glass, stopping twice to gauge the space left to the brim. When he set the bottle down she rose to stand over him and smooth his hair with her hand. She leaned and pressed her lips to his. A surge of panic swept over him but quickly passed when her mouth felt smooth and crystal-like. He pressed a hand against her shoulder, but her mouth parted against his and an inner warmth pushed past his lips and filled his chest till his whole being felt permeated with her. He embraced her and her tongue moved within his mouth and was startlingly warm. Currents of sensation swelled and ebbed within him in a sort of resonance with the strange woman he held. Eila broke the embrace and moved away. She pushed back her hair from her face and watched him as he rose unsteadily from his chair.

"Even without the external stimuli it was rather exciting," she said.

"I hadn't really believed you were like a human inside that jeweled exterior but that got high marks."

Eila shook her head and smiled. "I need to return to Tupa Inca; Drost is waiting. He's going to be very angry when he learns that the price has gone up for the beryllium. I hope he doesn't wish to make some drastic response."

Josiah shuddered. He'd better get word to Hector that he'd raised the price—not counting the bonus he intended for himself. Hector would be delighted with any increase, of course—except if he had knowledge of whom they were dealing with. Another thing bothered Josiah, what if he got out soon with a big payoff, but the hallucinations continued?

He didn't want to think about that, watching Eila. How could he feel a desire for such an unnatural creature? Was she real or was she and Drost somehow part of his hallucinations? That extra money destined for his retirement account might be needed to pay for assisted-living at some mental sanitarium.

"I've heard on the radio about an environmental society with Inca trappings popping up in major cities around the world," he said. "Know anything about that?"

Eila nodded, "I'd been planning to tell you about it before we were so pleasantly distracted. It's Drost's idea for spreading his slagging movement. He's taken some initial steps—slag conversions—at environmental conferences he's attended in several cities. Now he's planning to send me on an international trip to help build this new organization."

"And you're going?"

"There's no other choice for now; I shall have to, but first, Drost will need a small delivery of beryllium from you. One hundred kilos, and you must bring it here a week from today. And now, I've got to leave. Kepo, I've often heard you playing the shepherd's pipes on a quiet evening. I would like you to play for us before I go."

Kepo hurried to take down a bundled cluster of hollowed wood pipes from atop a shelf. He backed around Eila and out into the yard, where he sat on a stone bench. The plaintive, halting, skipping notes wafted into the still night air. A quarter-moon had risen above the peaks and gave outline to the house and sitting figures on the dimly lit mountainside. Presently, Eila rose and took the command module from her pocket. The Griffin descended seconds later and eased down onto the terrace. Eila shook out her flowing mane of silver hair and strode to the craft. Minutes later a dim, blue light glowed on the terrace. The Griffin lifted a few feet, held, and as the shepherd's pipes continued playing it soared off into the night.

CHAPTER 8—Holographs

In late afternoon Josiah paused in his climb and scanned the far upper peaks. The air had a cold bite and his breath steamed as he rested. What was happening up there? He'd made the small delivery of processed beryllium to Drost a week ago and had agreed to meet Eila today to provide a schedule and location for regular, future deliveries. He shook his head; the bizarre slagging venture had already begun and he hadn't been able to come up with any plan worthy of a so-called Galactic Druid. He wondered if he dared seek help. Could he organize some Indians to capture the Skatha and bury him alive as was done in the past? He squinted and his mouth twisted at the mere thought of it.

By early evening, he'd arrived at the cabin and sat with Kepo on the porch, watching the dim sunlight disappear behind the peaks. Kepo nudged his arm and pointed. A faintly glowing bluish green color flashed in the dusky sky, like the magnetic aura sometimes seen over the mountains. It dimmed momentarily in the gathering fog, and seconds later glowed above their terrace.

Josiah watched through the thin streamers of fog running across the ledge and saw the Griffin land. After a few minutes, Eila came into view through the thickening fog. She beckoned him to accompany her to the craft. He asked Kepo to wait for him in the cabin and joined her. All around the base of the Griffin small ports emitted jets of air pushing back the engulfing fog. Josiah followed her up into the Griffin. Inside, a walkway circled the wall perimeter, passing along a continuous desktop with monitoring screens and control panels set beneath the craft's observation windows.

She used her portable command module to shutter the observation windows, and close the hatchway.

"Access to the Griffin, flight activation, and navigation are controlled from this module," she said. "I have a few things to show you after I dock the module with the onboard computer and download my flight plan. I'm leaving tonight on a trip for the Inca Foundation and I want to stay away from the more heavily traveled air lanes and security zones. I want to avoid adding to flying saucer stories that may arise from chance observations. What have you to report, Josiah?"

"I don't have much," Josiah said. "The foundry is still tooling up to make a larger production run with the ore. What's been happening with the slagging?"

"Sit in one of those observation chairs and watch the area below us in the center of the craft and I'll explain as we go. Josiah turned a tracked chair out from the Griffin's control bench to sit and look down into a central pit area, where the walls and floor were finished in black.

That's the heart of the reconnaissance craft, our holographic surveilance arena," she said. "We can beam particle fields onto any target below, from altitudes up to 15,000 meters, and use our onboard computers to vary magnification, depth, and angle of the surveillance field." She flicked a switch at the arm of her chair and a large, grid-lined screen lit up on the floor of the arena. "The particles are tuned for precision layering of image," she said. "If a scanned individual or group seems of interest, the computer can lock in the coordinates and several hologram emitters are trained on the target. Our onboard projectors can then develop a three-dimensional hologram of the scene. I want to show you some observations taken on my last trip."

64

"It stores the data?"

"Yes, and you'll observe a serious flaw that has been discovered in our slagging program."

He leaned back in his chair. "A flaw, well, that is interesting. I've been thinking Drost's technology might be invincible. What happened?"

"Patience. We'll be looking at the hologram of a person who demonstrates the discovered flaw, and who now discomfits Drost immensely. She was his jewel when I first reported slagging her and showed him her hologram."

Josiah's expression caved, "You personally slagged her?"

"You're angry, but I didn't think I had any choice; for the time being we must do Drost's bidding or perish."

He looked at her warily, "How many other people have you slagged?"

"He wanted about thirty persons of international stature selected from among our Foundation members. I've done almost that, including this woman, a Middle Eastern government official named Vasthi. Most of the slags behave just as Drost expected, but Vasthi has been a puzzle."

"In what way?"

"In tests of absolute submission to Drost's commands, Vasthi seems to override her programmed response. She apparently possessed an extraordinary measure of freewill and motivation and seems to have retained at least some of these traits despite her slagging."

"Explain what you mean by that?" Josiah asked.

"I'll show you," she said, and flicked a switch. Josiah leaned forward to watch three figures materialize in the pit arena. "We'll be able to hear their voices, too," Eila said. "The holographic beams are modulated by the target's voice and the sound is reproduced by a computer in our projector system. The older of the two Arab men with Vasthi is a cabinet minister in another Middle Eastern state. The younger man is a stateless militia commander."

Josiah studied Vasthi—small in stature, a mass of tightly curling black hair, and dressed in khaki military blouse and trousers.

Eila noticed his interest. "If you'd like, we can focus in on her." She punched-in a format on her instrument panel and the figure of Vasthi grew in size, until only her head and shoulders filled the arena. Josiah stared in amazement at the gigantic bust as Eila dialed the holograph projector to rotate the holographic image. Vasthi continued speaking to her Arab companions as she turned to face Josiah. Large dark eyes and pale, full lips in a warm olive complexion. Responding to one of the men's voice, Vasthi's eyes narrowed and glinted with a hardness that straightened Josiah in his chair.

Vasthi said, "Your suicide squad of terrorists was responsible for the death of my dear friend, Breen. Those who survived capture will be imprisoned in solitary confinement for the rest of their lives. They should have been executed."

The unseen government official said in a distant voice, "But Madam Secretary, if you could only see your way clear for somehow releasing and spiriting my son out of your country. He is so young and did not weigh the gravity of joining the insurgents. I'm told that when his commander ordered him on this mission, he believed it was only to be for sabotage. I cannot believe he was among those who opened fire on your civilian bus."

Vasthi's face remained impassive as she turned to face another speaker.

The disembodied voice of the militia commander said, "I have given my word to the Minister that if you release his son, I will order a cessation of border raids by my militia for one year."

Vasthi scowled and was about to speak when the Minister interrupted.

"Please consider it, Madam Secretary. Much can be accomplished in that time to help stabilize the situation. The insurgents may gain their state peacefully. Your own state may grow in power and prosperity and be accepted in our region. This man's militia are not the only ones fighting you, but his withdrawal will surely make some difference and only for the price of releasing my son."

Eila dialed the controls to refocus Vasthi to life-size and recovered the images of the two Arab men. Vasthi rose from her seat at the table and addressed the two men.

"He will never be released, not in his lifetime," she said.

The militia chief spat on the floor. "Can the loss of a passing lover really be so non-negotiable? For the sake of this Breen you would hold our region to more rounds of bloodshed. *Inshallah*, so shall it be," he said.

The Minister rose, grim-faced, "Madam Secretary, please reconsider."

Vasthi stared at them, turned, and strode away from the table.

Eila switched off the holograph. "There you have it. Drost felt her programming was designed for her to have accepted a political bargaining, so that the Minister would have been indebted to her. She might then have counted on his restraint or collaboration in future power politics, such as cooperating in a brief, staged attack into his country to enhance her political stature in her own country."

"Maybe Drost presumed too much. How was the slagging mixture supposed to work?"

"The bio-metallic system he designed is much the same in principle as your own DNA and RNA molecules. Your DNA provides you with an evolutionary, genetic code needed for your survival, and your RNA molecule is the messenger that delivers the necessary code to your cells. Drost's slagging cocktail mimics that system. The beryllium strands contain his program, and the catalyst delivers messages to your RNA that selectively override the slags impulsive reactions incompatible with Drost's program, and reinforce or substitute slag reactions that will be compatible. Accordingly, the slag's daily behavior is partly freewill and partly Drost's programming."

"What caused Vasthi's deviation?" Josiah said.

"It would seem that perhaps Drost has underestimated the range of intensity in freewill among humans," she said. "This Vasthi is an extremely willful woman, and her personal genetic responses are compromising the slagged screen."

"What do you think Drost will do about it?"

"He doesn't know if the catalyst can be safely strengthened to control those slags who might have exercised such a superior level of freewill as Vasthi in their earlier life. He brooded about this and shut himself up in his laboratory for days. He must have decided something, because he now wishes to have our initial group of slags attend a special meeting. It will be held at a secluded retreat on the Galapagos Islands."

"Maybe he intends to kill Vasthi?"

"It's possible he may want her destroyed, but he could not do that himself. Like many Skatha, Drost has a Geise, a personal taboo. Breaking a Geise would extinguish the will of a Skatha to go on living. His Geise is never to slay a female of any race. If he wanted Vasthi, or me, destroyed, he would have to find some way of doing it that is not at his own hand." The light in Eila's eyes dimmed faintly at the frown that passed over Josiah's face. "Drost orders that you, too, are to attend the retreat. For what reason, I can't say, but I am worried."

CHAPTER 9—Island Retreat

Josiah walked along the black, sandy shore of the island. The tall lookout tower of an old buccaneer's fort rose from a rocky peninsula, and a gray, choppy sea spanned the horizon. Most of the summoned Foundation members had arrived in the Galapagos the previous day, and Josiah and the Skatha arrived that morning. Josiah stared at the slags when Eila introduced him at the lodge reception. He'd half-expected to see washed-out zombies, but during his earlier introductions they seemed graceful, intelligent people of some poise and charm. Vasthi appeared shortly before noon, arriving by a helicopter launched from a large military ship anchored some distance offshore. This had further fueled Drost's apprehensions about Vasthi.

The next morning Josiah walked along the sandy beach at the shoreline. A quarter mile later he encountered a rocky peninsula protruding a short distance into the ocean from higher ground. He climbed the peninsula and crossed it, crouching when he looked down and saw Vasthi ahead on the sandy beach. She wore a khaki military blouse and walking shorts and spoke with two men in black wetsuits and wearing diving tanks. After several minutes she dismissed the men and they entered the water and disappeared. Josiah's fascination with the woman grew and he felt he had to speak with her.

She turned as he loosened a shower of stones coming down the slope and watched as he came onto the beach and approached.

"Good Morning, Vasthi. A nice day, isn't it? I'm Josiah, we met at the reception." He was startled to see her take a small pistol from her bag and point it at him.

"You seem an unlikely assassin, so bubbly and cheerful at your work," she said.

"I'm a guest of the Foundation, just like you. I'd heard about you and hoped we'd have a chance to talk."

"A guest, not a member?"

"I haven't been tapped to join as a full-fledged member yet, but I have some business dealings relating to the Foundation, securing supplies and materials and such."

"What exactly is it that you heard about me?"

"Oh, the thumbnail sketch sort of thing—government official, tough soldier, beautiful woman, and Molecular Light rank in the Inca Foundation."

She smiled. "That much? What do you know of Molecular Light rank?"

"Only that it comes with a tremendous store of knowledge at the time of election, and requires an oath of loyalty and obedience to the Foundation principles and officers."

"You're a cautious individual, Josiah. I've noticed you speaking with Eila. She has seemed to me not only a clever environmental scientist, but also a very strange woman. I accept that this is a very ritualistic society, but does she always wear that Inca priestess mask at our gatherings?"

"I think you'll find out soon enough that it's no mask; she's from a different time and place, as is Drost whom you've yet to meet, though I shouldn't wonder if you question my mental facilities at this point."

"A year ago I would have thought you mad to have narrated such a story, but a lot has opened to me since then." She picked up a pouch left by the frogmen, slung the straps over her shoulders, and hooked her arm with Josiah's. "Come—I'll have to think more about what you've told me. A splendid name by the way, from the root, Joshua no doubt, though you don't look very Semitic. You'll join me in my quarters for some wine?"

They walked back the way Josiah had come, wading out a short distance to climb a low gap in the rock peninsula.

"Hang onto that pack and I'll give you a boost up," he said. He put his back to the rock and clasped his hands for a step hold. As she sprang up, a rolling wave caught him off balance and with a screech and shout both went tumbling into the water. Vasthi came up choking and gasping for breath while Josiah tried to steady her on her feet.

"No, stay where you are—enough. You may accomplish what dozens of terrorists could not," she said, in between coughs and gasps, holding him off with one hand while sluicing the water from her face and hair with the other. She stood and glared at him for a moment, and with a laugh and a shriek, she leaped to lock arms and legs about him. They tumbled beneath the surface of water, and both came up choking. They leaned over with hands resting on knees, trying to catch their breath while stilling their laughter.

Josiah clambered out of the water and onto the rocks and turned to take her pouch and lend her a hand up. They sat on top of the rock arm, drying in the soft breeze and hot sun. He watched as she threaded her hands through springy, coiled hair, billowing it out to dry. She smiled at him and started removing her soaked tunic.

"It would not be appropriate for a government undersecretary to arrive back at the center looking like a drowned cat, would it?" she said.

"Hardly." He watched as a bare-breasted Vasthi stood and removed her walking shorts. She spread her clothing on the rocks and began to unbutton his shirt.

"It might be healthier if we dry independently of our clothes, don't you think?" she said.

He pushed her hand away, "I can manage." He felt awkward to be following her lead. He discarded his outer shirt and as he peeled a tee shirt over his head, she loosened his belt and trousers. "Just a blessed second," he said, clutching the trousers' waistband and backing away, attempting to lift out a leg. He lost balance and teetered over and down the side of surf-slick boulders. With a cry and a bump down the rocks he fell into the water. Vasthi laughed, till she saw him buried by another wave while struggling with his trousers and dove in to help.

They swam back to the side of the rock arm and rested, standing on a submerged slab with the water lapping at their calves.

"Do you always act so insane?" he said, coughing and breathing deeply.

"The more I've seen of life the more reckless I've become," she said.

Josiah held her shoulders and kissed her. If it was meant to show a willing nature, it was little like the abandon she gave back. He struggled to keep his footing and keep her from tumbling them both into the water again. The sea broke noisily about the rocks and surged around their legs, and the occasional rogue wave left waterfalls spilling from the rocks above them.

By the time ardor had been spent, and minds were blissfully clearer, the incoming tide had crept in and the pocket of rock in which they stood was awash with foam from breaking waves.

"We've got to go," Vasthi said, as a high-rising wave ran along the rock and exploded into the pocket.

"Yes, probably not enough time left to have a proper talk about things," he said.

At the lodge, Josiah joined Vasthi in her quarters before the evening banquet. She wore a loose, high-neck white dress gathered in tightly around the waist with a gold-chained military medallion. She handed him a glass of deep red wine.

"Join me in a toast to Mannanan, god of the sea. Water is really your element, Josiah; we shall have to acquire a lover's retreat near the sea."

She moved to a wall switch and turned up the speed of the ceiling fan. The whir of the motor and oscillations of air spilling from the long, sweeping blades became more noticeable. "In case the walls are listening," she said, and drew Josiah down onto the couch beside her. They put their wine glasses on a table and kissed. He felt her shiver, or it was his own intensity of feelings for her. They separated and drank their wine quietly for several minutes.

"Let me tell you of my first encounter with Eila," she said. "And afterward, tell me everything you can about the significance of it, and what it foretells for the future."

The reminder of Eila's role in all of this troubled him, but then she'd pledged to help him—in a vague sort of way. He waited for Vasthi to go on.

"On that night, Breen and I—Breen was a former lover—went to a meeting of a new, environmental action and meditative group we'd heard about, the Inca Foundation. It was very popular at Breen's university. He was a lecturer at the university, and very much into environmental awareness, which I was, too. After the meeting, which seemed a blend of the occult and the inane, we sat about drinking wine with students, a few government workers, and the local director of the Foundation, a professor of marine biology. He asked me if I wanted to meet an exquisite woman who was one of the founders of the movement and who held one of the highest ranks in it. I was feeling quite giddy with wine and wanted to meet this woman. He took me immediately to another room which was very dark except for a lighted candle beside a seated figure. The professor left and closed the door behind him, and I remember resting my hand on my shoulder bag in case I had to gp for my pistol. It's the nature of living in a region of terrorism but I was determined to show no fear.

"'You tremble, Vasthi,' she said to me.

"'Why should I? You are mistaken,' I said, 'and why are

76

we talking to each other in this darkness? Turn on some proper lighting so that I might see a woman who has attained a state of Molecular Light.' She seemed to me to be masked. 'If you are as exquisite as I'm told I might take you as a lover,' I said and laughed afterward, but she remained silent for an awkward few moments.

"'You're an impetuous woman, a very physical creature,' she said. 'Let me rest my eyes a few minutes longer and I'll turn up the lights. Join me now in a glass of wine and we will speak more openly with each other.'

"I took the glass of wine she offered and hesitated. She let out a strange, tinkling laughter and I was uncomfortable, uncertain. I drank impulsively and was about to reach out and shake some respect into this pretentious creature but the emptied glass slipped from my hand and crashed to the floor. I'd drunk too much, I thought, and I watched dumbly as she rose from her chair.

"'You are the sort of leader the Foundation searches for,' she said. 'I've listened to you and observed you closely tonight. I knew you were a candidate for the highest honor of Molecular Light even before I was informed of your high position in your government.'

"She came to me, leaned her arms across my shoulders, and brought her face close to mine. My eyes were clouded over, but she seemed such a strange creature. An awesome, jewel-like luminescence played over her mask as she drew me close to her. I felt immobile. She lingered a moment with cool lips on my cheek and then kissed me full on the lips."

Vasthi sweated despite the whirring fan. She took out a

handkerchief and wiped it over her face. "I wanted to push her away, Josiah, but I was powerless. Surges of excruciating pain shot through me but I remained mute, unable to cry out. I began to lose consciousness and might have collapsed but she held me and kept her mouth pressed to mine. I don't know how long she held me but when it was over I was still on my feet. I remember an unprecedented feeling of great vitality and assurance. I saw this woman in a new light. I started to think of her as someone I'd been waiting to serve all my life, but this warred against other feelings I had of needing to reassert myself. We sparred with words; she with imperious commands on how I was charged to seek power so that I might better serve the Foundation. I held back, evasive at times, non-committal, as much as I dared, still trying to remain myself."

"You drank a consciousness-altering catalyst, and she made you a slag," Josiah said.

"A slag?" Vasthi whispered. "I didn't understand what had happened. I suspected I was drugged with the wine and she'd imposed some sort of mind-control over me. It was very strange. I was filled with energy when I returned to my office that night. Problems that had stunned me before became as clear as day. Complicated logic, equations of probability for options in developing a nuclear strike force suddenly became no more than simple propositions. Moreover, I glimpsed parallels from ancient through modern history revealing strengths and weaknesses of our own political options that had not been so evident before."

Josiah leaned forward and refilled their wine glasses on the table. "The wine you drank that night held a mind-altering beryllium substance, that may or may not be permanent."

She leaned back on the couch and held a hand to her brow. "So I've been swept into a rather awesome cult seeking some sort of absolute power over its members." She dropped her hand and turned to look at him. "What is your part in all of this?"

He ran his fingers through his hair. "I have a little trouble sorting out facts from fantasy. You may be dealing with lunatics from two different worlds."

"Go on; you've forgotten I have an extraordinary capacity for assimilating and analyzing difficult data since my initiation into the Foundation. Perhaps I can give you some insights into a proper sorting of your facts and fancy."

He gave her a wry smile. "Well, the facts started with my intention of augmenting my old-age pension with a share of an enormous rip-off of beryllium ore. I discovered the ore in a power plant excavation and threw-in my lot with a government official who helped manage the required illegal moving and processing of the ore. About the same time I began having epileptic seizures complete with visions that sought to persuade me I'd had an earlier existence. In the visions I was charged with destroying creatures described as beryllium eaters, who have in fact turned out to be Drost and Eila. It seems now I have no choice but to accept my role in this kabuki drama."

He related the little he knew of the Skatha, their damaged world, the expeditions launched into space and the arrival of one of the spaceships here, their experiences as the fire-tongue allies of the Incas, the sacrifices, all that he knew of events until now.

"By all that is sacred," she whispered. "And now I've

joined you in your kabuki. I've heard Drost mentioned by Eila; he appears to be the more powerful?"

"Yes, he's the one in control; the Inca Foundation and the slagging venture were his creations. Eila wanted no part of it but she's afraid of him. I have a major, supernatural awe of him myself. I tried to destroy him in an excavation blast, but it didn't even faze him. I'm hoping to get another chance but it's got to be successful or I could be in serious difficulty with him."

"In the total scheme of things, do you think it really possible that you might have been reincarnated as a Druid?"

"I'm working with that premise. It's a better choice than giving in to despair, but my seizure visions haven't shown any signs of relenting. It's kind of a Joan of Arc thing with me—I've been called and I'm going along with the call."

"Good. It might be better if you'd been given a few extraordinary powers to aid you, but together we may be able to overcome the Skatha."

"Well, Drost anyhow; Eila just wants out."

"So she told you. We'll see."

Vasthi rose and paced the room. She returned abruptly and sat beside him. "The thought of that insidious metallic compound in my body frightens me," she said. "Still, it seems to have had no deleterious effects. On the contrary, it's increased my intellectual powers to match those of any mortal alive and even my physical strength feels magnified. Thankfully, I've completely obliterated any initial feelings of subservience toward the Skatha. I feel I'm as completely in charge of my will power as I've always been."

80

"They suspect as much," Josiah said. "That's why Drost summoned you and the other slags to this meeting."

Vasthi's face darkened. "What does he mean to do about it?"

"I don't know but he appears to have something in mind," he said.

"Let him try what he will. He'll find one slag that is more than his match."

CHAPTER 10—Slag Creation

After dining that evening, Foundation members were shown into the meeting room by Indian servants brought from Tupa Inca. This wing of the lodge projected into a sand-filled estuary, eroded into the lava rock by ancient, heavy seas. Small, wood-framed windows with salt encrusted panes stood at eye level, just above the ground line. A storm roiled the sea, and heavy surf pounded the nearby beach.

The impatient slapping of a wood gavel brought Josiah's attention back from watching the sea and he took a seat beside Vasthi. Drost, wearing the guise of another recent victim, a professorial-looking man with a sallow complexion, with a full beard and moustache, stood behind a long, wooden table at the head of the room. An array of electronic equipment was lying on the table.

"The First International Congress of the Inca Foundation will come to order, ladies and gentlemen, please," Drost said in his deep, resonant voice. Thirty slags, men and women from several continents, disengaged from small, conversational groups and took their places in the rows of seats.

Drost introduced himself as the Executive Secretary of the Foundation and congratulated them on their selection as Molecular Light members. "During the two weeks we shall meet here," Drost said, "we will conduct workshops in addition to pursuing organizational matters. I'm sure you're all going to find the workshops extremely interesting."

Josiah glanced over at Vasthi. She seemed calm, even

amused.

Drost leaned forward on the lectern and delivered a stunning revelation of the biochemical transformation of intellectual powers that had occurred during their initiation into the Foundation. More than one of the initiates gasped audibly. "Rest assured," Drost continued, "it was all for the good of the planet, and would add to their own honor." He avoided mention of their controlled obedience to him. All were by now aware of the dramatic personal transformations they'd undergone since initiation, but they'd hardly dared to question one another about such transformations. Regardless, he had their complete attention now. They'd anticipated from the moment of setting foot on the island that they were called there to meet such a messianic figure.

Eila entered the room and went to sit beside Drost at the speaker's table. A hushed silence descended on the room. Those who had been initiated by Drost did not recognize him in his new guise, but others remembered the mysterious woman in the Inca priestess's mask who had initiated them. Tonight, she wore all black, a military style, pressed tunic and trousers. Her flowing, silvery hair framed a small portrait of her gem-like features. It was the first time any of them had seen her quite this clearly and they wondered anew about her appearance.

Drost introduced Eila as the Chief Operations Officer of the Foundation. "We, then, are your creators and mentors," he said, "the holders of absolute truth, which we shall deliver to you. You have been ordained as our warriors—slags--in the lexicon of an ancient world. Each of you has been reborn into positions of new, greater powers, and each has embarked on a sacred campaign to promulgate a new order on this planet."

84

"What a pompous fool," Vasthi whispered to Josiah.

Drost seemed to have noticed her diversion, but he went on, "You might wonder at the boldness of our campaign. How will such a small number of leaders and slags gain the ascendancy and dominance in our society? Even if Eila and I continued adding to your ranks, might not it take as long and meet with as little lasting success as other world empires? Consider those led by Christ, the Prophet Mohammed, Lenin, Henry Ford,,,"

Vasthi looked at Josiah and rolled her eyes upward.

"You can be sure we considered the huge challenges when we designed your biochemical transformation," Drost said. "We've endowed you with the capacity to be co-creators of other slags. You have only to learn to use these capabilities and it is one of the lessons you will need to master before leaving here to return to your own countries."

Vasthi nudged Josiah, "Co-creators of other soldiers— now there's a strategy that may be of interest."

"A second lesson which must be brought home to you during this conference," Drost went on, "is painful for us to have to mention. We created an elevated form of existence in you and you owe us love, honor, and obedience. You cannot hope to hide any shortcomings in your duties. You will learn that your leaders are omniscient in all things concerning our slags—"

"Especially when he has that bitch Eila dashing about the world checking up on us," Vasthi whispered.

"Pride, envy, and arbitrary use of freewill are sins against your new nature. These are vices from your old, imperfect state of being and must be expunged from your new selves. We shall expose any such lingering vices with an annual ritual that will help purge our ranks of any corrupted individuals."

Some of the audience had seemed to be in a somber state of acceptance of all they were hearing, but now they began to look agitated and whispered among themselves.

Josiah placed his hand over Vasthi's, "I think this is all about you, and he's had plenty of time to plan things. Maybe you ought to signal your ship to come in and get you. I need to stay and go along with everything until I can find some way of carrying out my own mission."

Vasthi had maintained a calm appearance, giving rapt attention to all of Drost's words. "We shall see who will win out in a contest between them and me," she whispered. "I have no fear of the Skatha or their threatened ritual."

"We shall deal with correction and punishment of willful vices later," Drost said. "On a more positive side, we will now demonstrate the powers of the Molecular Light priesthood, whereby you may become co-creators of a new race. Your new powers will make you the ruling class of your world. We will start with a few readings from the ancient Book of the Skatha. It is a world from which we have come to help you build a new and better life. The book's teachings comprise the received theology of your new priesthood. After the readings we shall ordain you into the creative ability you will share with us."

A switch flicked, and the room plunged into darkness. A lectern light snapped on at one side of the long table, illuminating the head and shoulders of Eila as she stood and read from a book on the lectern.

"In the beginning there was pure consciousness throughout. In the first law of Universal Being it was made known that consciousness is an inherent property of mass, but it may be lost or diminished by escape of energy from the mass. This is known as the law of Universal Decay, against which consciousness rebels, with all the resources it can command.

"In the beginning, Aquama coalesced from the streams of consciousness existing in the Galaxy. No other coalescence in the universe matched that of Aquama; she was the jewel of creation. Through the ages, the noble consciousness of Aquama remained undiminished, owing to a constant influx of energy from the emissions of its twin-star satellites.

"In those days the godhead of the Galactic Consciousness was represented by the Macnessa, the sacred bio-metallic phalluspods which sprouted in temple gardens outside each city. In the early days the Skatha tasted of the Macnessa on the Night of Oracles, and were then able to commingle their own consciousness with that of the Macnessa, the universal consciousness. It was thus that the oracles of the godhead were delivered for observance over the following year. It was in this way, too, that those who had been unfaithful to earlier oracles were poisoned by their tasting of the Macnessa." Eila paused and looked out into the darkened room.

"Obviously Drost will use some form of that mythology to cower us into submission, but just let him try," Vasthi whispered to Josiah. "Bio-metallic phalluspod, indeed."

The distant thunder of surf on the beach intruded on

Josiah's attention to Eila's words. The story of the early exploits of the Skatha, the decline of the planet Aquama as it lost its energy source, and the resurgence of the dying Skatha as a bio-metallic race, was dimly familiar. He noticed Vasthi leaning intently forward now, absorbing all that Eila had to say, digesting and analyzing all that the story might reveal about the strengths and weaknesses of their Skatha adversaries, and what it implied of her own new nature as a slag.

She turned and whispered to him, "Why is it you haven't been slagged like the rest of us?"

"That was Drost's intention on a previous occasion, but I had a seizure first. He and Eila detected aberrant brain wave patterns in me during my seizure, which Eila said revealed I was a Galactic Druid. She said slagging would probably kill me and kept him from trying to slag me."

"Do you think he might still do it anyway?"

"I don't think he wants to take the chance—yet. He needs the beryllium and I'm his key for quickly securing it."

Eila concluded her narrative and the lights came back on.

Drost stood and walked behind the electronic apparatus on the table. "We will now demonstrate the powers we have bestowed on you as slags," he said. Afterward, you shall be able to slag others into our fold. May I have a volunteer from our audience, please?" There were no immediate volunteers, and then Vasthi's hand shot up. He seemed to force himself not to look her way, but faltered to locate any other candidate, and kept returning to stare at her upraised hand. Finally, he chose her.

"Let us start with one of our more illustrious priestesses. Vasthi, will you come up here, please?"

Vasthi looked around and smiled, rose, and walked to the table. Eila motioned her into a chair and, as Drost explained the procedure to his audience, Eila taped tiny electrodes on wires to Vasthi's lips, temples, and wrists.

"In order for Vasthi to build the electro-biotic charge potential between her billions of internal, polarized beryllium strands needed for the transformation of a new slag, she must be trained," Drost said. "We will use bio-feedback, which some of you may already have used for controlling alpha waves in the brain and lowering breathing and pulse rates during your Incan meditation practices. Vasthi will use similar feedback from our specialized sensors to monitor the process of aligning her internal beryllium strands and the accompanying buildup of her electrical charge. The alignment is a programmed organic function of muscular dilation and contraction done in sequence with pulse control. She'll watch this pair of green and yellow lights and try to optimize her performance to keep moving the needle forward in the yellow range. The headphones Eila is placing over Vasthi's ears will help her control her breathing rate as she tries to smooth a beating audio tone that accompanies needle movement. The level of charge she must reach for slagging will be noted when this needle moves into the red band of its operating range."

Eila whispered a few instructions to Vasthi, who signaled she was ready. It took a few seconds for Vasthi to move the needle off its zero peg, and soon the needle began to flicker back and forth between the green and yellow zones. The yellow feedback light soon came on for longer periods and the charge needle moved farther into the yellow range. A few momentary collapses backward and then the charge needle moved steadily forward—but excruciatingly slow—and Vasthi's clasped hands on the table trembled with impatience. Eila placed a hand on her shoulder and eased her back onto her chair. The needle rose more rapidly now and finally, with a rumble of approval from the audience, it crossed into the red range.

Eila reached and grasped Vasthi's wrist, and raised her hand up toward her lips. Drost dimmed the lights, and though Vasthi struggled against Eila's imposition, her hand moved closer to her lips. As her fingers touched her lips, a flashing blue-green light enveloped her figure. Drost turned the lights back up and Eila helped straighten the slumped figure of Vasthi from the table back onto her chair.

"That was a relatively low level of energy discharge," Drost said, "compared to what can be achieved through a little more practice. Be aware that one pole of your charge concentrates at body extremities, and the other pole at the mucous membranes, as with fingertips and lips, for example. Your sudden discharge into a slag initiate is the fire-kiss of initiation and installs his or her program onto the beryllium strands swallowed in a ceremonial drink . The fire-kiss is related to a more intimate sacrament that can be executed only by Skatha, called fire-tonguing, which we needn't go into at this time."

Of course he's not going to talk about that, Josiah thought.

Drost said, "Vasthi has been an apt pupil. I hope the rest of you will do as well during your next week of training. Before leaving the island, each of you will receive a quantity of the slagging catalyst, enough for initiating six candidate slags, and you will receive instructions for identifying attributes desirable in your candidates. It is no small honor to be found worthy of initiation into our Foundation."

"Will we be taught how to prepare additional catalyst for future recruitments?" Vasthi asked, rising from her chair with help from Eila.

Drost stopped arranging papers on the table and looked over at her. "Of course not, Vasthi; furnishing the catalyst for a soul awakening is the concern only of your leaders. It is enough that you are enabled to spark the requisite souls into being at our direction."

Vasthi leaned with a hand on the edge of the table. "We would be able to create more slags if we had larger supplies of the catalyst is all I'm saying."

"That won't be necessary. The elect of the priesthood is planned to be small, but carefully chosen," he said. "With perhaps only 5,000 of the elect we shall have sufficient numbers to make our influence felt over the masses of this world." He frowned at the impertinent look on Vasthi's face, sorted through more notes on the table, and looked out at his audience. "We shall celebrate The Night of the Macnessa in two days from now. You have heard all you need to know about the ritual in the readings by Eila. Prepare yourselves in your own way for this night of past atonement and future beginnings. May the Macnessa be merciful to the unfaithful," he said in a solemn tone, and walked from the room.

CHAPTER 11—Vasthi & Eila

Later that night Vasthi walked with Josiah along the beach. A low, oblate moon gave an eerie light to the island's strange plant life along the beach. They stopped and she took his hand. "I need to press Eila for more information on the technical process of producing and programming the beryllium strands and catalyst."

"I don't get it. Why would you need to know that?"

"Josiah, love, you're distressed." She watched him quietly for a few moments. "Look, if I could understand the technology of this process I might be able to undo certain insidious effects the slagging has induced but still retain its best effects. My countries intelligence service could help me identify everyone here, and I could get in touch with them later. And have you forgotten that his programming is doing battle within my own psyche? I've coped with it and mastered it so far but who knows whether it might still subdue me, and make me subservient to that manic slob. Would you abandon me to that?"

He was uncomfortable with her stratagem and watched her, a diminutive goddess of battle, hands on hips, white gown whipping in the sea breeze. "I'm not too optimistic Eila will tell us anything, and why would she?" he said.

Vasthi tilted her head back, clapped her hands, and laughed. "Josiah, Josiah, you can't be serious? Though our beryllium woman's heart is entombed in metal, the glow in her eyes when she looks at you is sign enough of her feelings for you. She will tell you anything."

Josiah looked out over the ocean and remained silent.

"I'm not asking you to betray Eila," she said. "I'm asking you to help me." She put her arm around him and leaned against him. "You've told me that her plan was totally different than Drost's, and I believe that. But excepting perhaps for you, she has a loyalty to Drost more than to anyone or anything else. The other slags and I mean little to her. You've said she wants to leave this planet and return to her own world, but now that she's fallen in love with you, and believe me, she has, how will she resolve her dilemma? She's perhaps put both herself and us at risk, and what's the point? A physical relationship between you is either impossible or surely some electro-mechanical marvel?"

The twisted expression on his face made her laugh. "If the opportunity comes to make love with her, take it," she said. "I'll understand, and it may be something to tell our grandchildren about." She locked her arms around his neck and kissed him and pulled him down to kneel together on the warm, black sand. "You've become so rigid—what's troubling you?"

"So many things are piling up, the oath I've taken to a mystical shade during my seizures, feeling some sort of bond with an alien woman, leaping into a relationship with you. I'll only bring more complications into your life."

A moan escaped her lips. She pushed him back into a seated position, turned and flopped onto her back with her head in his lap. "You're too scrupulous by far," she said. "Never mind, I'll learn your moods and ways and together we'll defeat Drost."

They lay quietly for a long time, until Josiah eased out

94

from under her and helped her to her feet. "Let's go see Eila," he said. "'She's going to be stunned when you propose we all join together in toppling Drost."

"I'm so glad," she said. "You had me worried. What's your best guess as to whether she'll help us?"

"It's hard to say how far she'll go to defeat Drost's ambitions. She might not have opposed him if he'd been a little less malevolent, but she seemed to draw the line when he began his slagging venture."

"His fire-tonguing orgies should have disturbed her just as much."

"Hard to argue that. She hasn't been mankind's greatest benefactor, but then I don't think she's ever pretended she was."

"At least she'll have a chance now to best Henry Ford," Vasthi said

Josiah stopped walking and looked at her, but she laughed and caught at his arm. "Let's go, Eila awaits," she said.

It was almost midnight when Eila greeted them in a robe and led them into her study. "What is the occasion of this late call, Josiah? Might it have something to do with this illustrious and beautiful priestess of the Molecular Light? But come, sit, and I will have a servant pour us drinks."

She left the room as Josiah and Vasthi settled into highly polished, heavy wood armchairs facing a stone fireplace. An Indian servant entered and placed another chair beside them. He left and returned with a tray of drinks. When Eila came back she'd changed into a narrow, satiny black dress reaching to the floor. The flicker of the fire played in dancing lights across her thin, gemstone face. She sank carelessly into her chair and took a sip from her drink.

"What is it you wished to talk about, Josiah?" she said.

He emptied his glass. "To begin with, Vasthi and I have become close—"

Eila interrupted, "In only two days? Well, I'm impressed, my dear Vasthi."

"Human love can be like that—spontaneous, intense, without any need for a preconditioning of time," Vasthi said.

"Very inspirational—you were saying, Josiah?"

"I've told Vasthi of your distaste for Drost's world scheme and your plan to return—"

"You were wrong to speak of such things with her," Eila said, and she got up and faced Josiah. He grimaced and set his glass down. She whirled away and paced the room. "Really, Josiah, you have placed us both in grave danger. What I told you was meant for you only. If Drost were to find out about this, he would have us destroyed immediately. How could you betray my trust in you?"

"Perhaps we can join in a plan that will help all three of us attain our goals," Vasthi said.

"And exactly what is this plan?" Eila said.

"To regain control of my own destiny and to help my compatriots regain control of theirs."

"I wasn't aware you were having any difficulty in keeping control of your own singular destiny," Eila said.

"At the moment I'm my own person," Vasthi said. "But I wonder what effect time will play in weakening my willpower over the programming of those strands and screening power of the catalyst."

"So, you've also been told of such things," Eila said, glancing a moment at Josiah. "What is it that you propose?"

"Teach me the technology involved in producing the programmed strands and the catalyst."

"I see; and what do you give me in return?" Eila said.

Vasthi waited, and Josiah spoke up. "Help in securing the beryllium for your world."

Eila looked at Josiah for a long time and the play of light dimmed on her features. "I'd already counted on you for such help. Perhaps I had other unrealistic expectations of you, also. Now that we've discussed Vasthi's and my goals, at least those we feel free to state at this time, perhaps we should revisit your goals. You've come to at least tacitly accept your incarnation as a Galactic Druid with a mission of destroying Drost. How do I know you don't plan to destroy me also?"

"Of course I wouldn't, but I'm getting worried. You said you haven't ever fire-tongued anyone but you've been helping Drost set up his Foundation, and you've made slags of quite a few people."

"Drost was appointed commander of our expedition and I don't think I've had any choice but to take his orders, ever, from the very beginning of our landing here. As for my slagging ventures, consider that Drost's, forty bureaucrats have been given the minds and impulses of some of Earth's historic, intellectual or ruling giants. Of course what they do with their powers depends a great deal on the leadership imposed by Drost, since they're programmed to seek power on his behalf. Without him, they'd be on their own, as indeed their mentors from the past had been. How well that might turn out may depend on those mentors' intellects, would it not?"

"I guess we'd have to see; but meanwhile you're saying it has to be up to me to remove Drost from the equation?" Josiah said.

"A fitting challenge for a Galactic Druid, is it not?"

He lifted his arms in the air and let them fall. "Will you help Vasthi find a way to overcome her slagging? Show her what's involved in the technology. Maybe she's got the mind to handle it."

"There is little I wouldn't have tried to do for you, Josiah, but to ask this for a woman I trust no more than Drost—I cannot," she said.

He turned to Vasthi, "I guess that's it."

Vasthi smiled. "Patience, Josiah. We are dealing with intense emotions all around. We'll have a few drinks with Eila, and she may think differently of it in time."

Eila's voice seemed tired, "Yes, Josiah, stay a while longer and don't be angry."

The three sat drinking, quietly, speaking now and then of

other countries Eila had visited on her Foundation trips and had found so different from South America. For every three glasses of wine Josiah and Eila drank, Vasthi drank but one. The two women parried in their words, Vasthi in a greater knowledge of people and the environmental changes they drove in the world, and Eila, in a greater sense of wisdom about the psychological and physical interdependency of all things.

Josiah rose to his feet, unsteady. "I've had it; I need to get some sleep. Are you coming, Vasthi?"

"Not just yet," she said. "Eila is a fascinating person and I must make the most of this opportunity to speak of the many things in which we share an interest."

"We shall talk more if you wish," Eila said. "But first, I must say good night to Josiah." She rose from her chair, steadied herself a moment with her hand on the table edge, and took Josiah by the arm. She showed him through the short hallway and out onto the porch.

"You must not be angry with me," she said, standing with him in dim starlight and a moist, warm breeze. "I would not see you harmed even if it meant my own existence, but I cannot do what you asked for the sake of a temporary affair between you and this woman. I trust her no more than she trusts me. Be wary of her, Josiah. But enough of her, look at me." She laid her hand alongside his face. "I've never worn a sheath, but would you care more for me if I did?"

"No, I wouldn't want you to do that," he said. "You're a strange being, but there's an awesome beauty about you, too." He ran the tips of his fingers down her face, her lips, and her throat. Something between the feel of silk and cut diamond, he imagined, in the headiness of his drinking. He tried to look steadily into her eyes but could not hold a focus. "I've got to go," he said. "If you can help Vasthi, I'd be indebted to you."

"Good night, Josiah," she said, and turned to go back inside.

CHAPTER 12—The Macnessa

The next morning Josiah was still groggy after a ten-minute hot shower. He wandered to the beach in a warm sun and moderate breeze, and walked in the sand. The breeze helped lift his spirits and he strode briskly for a few miles. When his head had cleared, he made his way back to the dining room. Vasthi was there drinking coffee at a table and he joined her.

"How did it go?" he said.

"She's a hard-to-read woman."

"Aren't you all?"

"No more than some men I know," and she touched her coffee cup to his. "Things look promising though," she said.

After breakfast they returned to the meeting room of the previous day. Drost opened the morning session with a lecture on the Machiavellian principles of acquiring and using power, and his lecture was liberally spiced with shrewd observations and anecdotes on the nature of man, particularly as exemplified by his idiosyncratic model, Henry Ford. The afternoon continued with individual training in the techniques of slagging.

At dinner that night, Vasthi spoke guardedly with Josiah. "Our time is growing short; we've got to find out more about what Drost plans for tomorrow's Night of the Macnessa. The lights have been on in the top of the stone tower for the past two nights, and I suspect that's where Drost's odious creature is being reborn."

"Maybe you should get some of your ship's frogmen back here for your protection," he said. "I was thinking this morning of how I must be a big disappointment to the Druid fraternity. Do you still find any of what I've told you about being a Druid believable?"

"All my reflections and intuition suggest it could be so. The signs are so numerous. You arrived in this corner of the world at a fortuitous time. You discovered the beryllium ore and drew the Skatha into revealing their presence. Cosmic forces entered your consciousness through a little understood, supernaturally inferred disorder of the human brain, and the message is always the same: destroy Drost."

"Don't remind me of the seizures. I've been lucky not to have any lately. Maybe they figure I'm at least trying, but I was thinking about something you said. Akla should have allowed me some special powers or arcane craft to do my job. I have this sickening, debilitating fear whenever I'm even near Drost. I'm afraid I'm going to fail miserably and wind up like a latex mask stretched over his hulking frame."

"We have each other to depend on now. I don't fear him at all, and I'll help you destroy him." Her eyes narrowed, "but first, I'll need to learn more of his science of slagging if I'm to help myself and the others."

Josiah shuddered. Once started along that path, where would it end? There were times he felt less at ease with Vasthi than with Eila.

"We'll go together to the tower this evening," she said. "We've got to find out what he's up to, and perhaps we'll learn how to oppose this demon of destruction he's creating. I'd like to delay any confrontation though, until I find out more about the strands and catalyst from Eila."

"All right let's get on with it," Josiah said.

Near one A.M. two figures moved in close to the base of the sixty-foot high stone tower at the corner of the compound. A low stonewall corridor connected it at its base with the living quarters taken by the Skatha within the compound. Stone rubble littered the ground around the tower.

"You want us to try scaling that?" Josiah said, looking up. "I don't think I can."

"You can do it; I've shown you how to use the climbing gear I got from the ship. I'll climb in the lead and set anchor clips. Don't worry about the climbing part. Those stone blocks look so uneven it'll be like going up a ladder. Here, belay this line for me; I'm starting up."

She flipped the loop of light nylon rope over her shoulder and around her back. Scrambling up the wall a few blocks, she swung her rock pick at a mortar joint above her and installed a clip. Climbing higher, she surveyed the wall above and broke out another seating for a clip. Working rapidly, she rose higher, spooling out the nylon rope and setting clips until she was about twenty feet above Josiah.

"Begin," she called down. "You can do it."

"Yeah, easy for you to say when you've probably already practiced the whole routine in a commando school." He hooked up to the line she'd secured with anchor clips, and looked up to where she waited, locked off to an anchor. He rose steadily, feeling for each new finger hold, each toe hold, gaining confidence but sweating and trembling each time he rose past another anchor clip. He forbade himself to think. It was probably impossible to fall with her ready to secure him against the top anchor. Think—he was in good shape and it was just another stressful, physical job. His arm trembled as he let go each handhold and reached for the next higher one. Rise on a toehold—feel—grip. As he approached Vasthi, she unhooked from her anchor and resumed climbing in the lead.

The next segment of the climb went a little faster, but tiring. The wind became alarmingly strong at forty feet above the ground. His breath came in short gasps as much from fear as from exertion. He paused to look seaward and that was calming. He didn't seem that high above the moonlit whitecaps breaking in the surf zone. Hesitantly, he looked below, caught his breath, and wrenched his head back up. He stared a few moments at the next higher clip to steady his nerves, and resumed climbing. Rise—feel—grip, and on the next lift-off. He extended his arm as high as he could reach and darted his hand left and right searching for the next grip.

"I'm stuck," he called in a rasping voice. "I can't reach anything."

"Stay calm and keep your voice down. When the wind stills our voices carry. I've taken up the slack. Hug the face and try for a higher toe hold with your other foot."

He was going to shout it was impossible, and his foot found a knobby protrusion on a higher stone block. He moved up quickly and kept climbing to avoid giving himself time to think about his swelling fear. The strong wind tore at his jacket and his collar end slapped at his face. When he'd reached near to Vasthi's toehold she began climbing again. He hugged the tower wall as she swung her pick into a joint and sent sprays of mortar showering down on him. He looked out to sea again and waited for her to reach the next anchoring point. When he looked up again she was nowhere in sight.

"What the hell?"

As he strained to see, her head and shoulders appeared over a stone wall and she tugged at the nylon line, jerking her head to signal him to finish coming up. She'd made it to the top landing. He took a deep breath, it was impossible to fall, and he extinguished his rampant doubt and climbed. The stone seemed more polished and slick at this height and the wind buffeted and clawed at him each time he leaned out from the face. Rise—feel—grip. He mouthed it like a mantra as he jacked himself up the wall. His fingertips grew sore from searching the coarse, mortared joints for grip holds. Don't think—do. His footing slipped on a stone face, and though he still had a handgrip, his heart hammered. He felt the reassuring tightening on the climbing rope, and he renewed his efforts. A few more feet of climbing and Vasthi gripped his shoulder and helped him up over the edge and onto the landing.

"That wasn't too bad, was it?" she said, her face exuberant.

"Stimulating—like drilling holes in my own kneecaps.

What have we got up here?" They crouched on a narrow stone-cobbled ledge surrounding the lookout room, and the wind thrummed noisily past them. A sweep of dimly lit, salt-encrusted windows faced out to sea and they crept to the edge of the windows. Inside, a single large room, circular, with cement-plastered walls and containing electronic consoles and machinery positioned throughout. The lighting inside was dim.

"They're both in there," Vasthi whispered. She took a small amplifier from her pack, pressed a suction cup pickup to the window, and passed one of the two sets of wireless earphones to Josiah.

"That's an odd-looking heap on the platform next to Drost," Josiah said.

"Yes, watch closely. Did you see it move?"

Eila stood in the shadows away from the raised platform in the center of the room. A huge, stella-flux magnascan lifted slowly above the platform. Drost stepped back from the electronic test console at which he'd been working and studied the bio-metallic phalluspod standing on the platform. Superficially, it resembled a toadstool. The shaft of the phalluspod was pocked with yawning, sucking orifices. Below, the shaft opened out into a standing base of undulating, wormlike tentacles on which it balanced. The top of the shaft was crowned with a wrinkled, leathery dome. A shining, obsidian black orb stared out from the domed head. A jerking, rotational movement of the head as it turned its black orb to scan the room brought a wide smile to Drost's borrowed face.

"I believe it's been a huge success, Eila," he said. "The

106

last dosage of magnetic flux has activated our Macnessa's consciousness." The voice in the earphones was scratchy and Vasthi adjusted the squelch. Drost signalled to Eila, "Unhook the methane tube from its digestive vent. We shall see if the animus of our child is self-sustained."

"I'd prefer not to go anywhere near this rank abomination," Eila said.

"You're too finicky; I'll untether our child myself," he said, and stepped onto the platform. The Macnessa made a hissing sound and exhaled a cloud of fulsome vapor as it backed away from his approach. Drost roared with laughter.

"See how it fears its father, Eila. Look at the malevolent eye it fixes on me." Drost began to choke on the Macnessa's fumes and shielded his nose and mouth with his hand. His features glinted with delight as he grabbed for the plastic tube curling from an appendage on the Macnessa's shaft, linking it to the methane synthesizer. With a quick wrench, Drost tore the feeding tube free from the Macnessa. The creature let out a stifled cry and lurched at him. It attempted to suck his outstretched arm into one of its orifices. With a loud roar Drost drew back his arm and struck the Macnessa with such force that goblets of ooze flew from it across the room. The creature withdrew slightly and appeared to tense for another rush at Drost. The black orb flashed and shook in its head. Its orifices strained and gulped and fumes shot out as if driven by an air bellows, but Drost stood his ground. With a shriek, the Macnessa flew forward on its slithering, tentacles.

Drost drew his weapon. Using a fanning motion of one hand to cock the intensity slide, he aimed from the waist and activated. A lighted beam, surrounded by misty white vapors, stabbed through the air. A shrieking sob came from an open, hairy slit in the Macnessa's shaft and the domed head quivered.

"Enough, Master, stay your freezing ray," it cried. "I feel I am slipping back into that terrible, sleeping world of stone. Spare me, and I will serve you well."

Drost deactivated his heat-sink gun and laughed in triumph. The Macnessa quieted, and a milky white membrane shuttered the orb. The orifices yawned in rippling sequence over the surface.

"That's better, my foul offspring. You do well to act docile before your creator," Drost said.

"Now that you've tamed your monster perhaps you will finish telling me of its conception," Eila said.

"It will be a pleasure, my dear. It mimics the Macnessa of our old world, but with a little biochemistry it goes beyond that. The idea for our creature came about from my interest in the evolutionary history of Earth, a history more complex even than Aquama. I was particularly interested in the period of the great magnetic storm caused by the explosion of the comet, Corso, inside Earth's galaxy. It was responsible for the disappearance of a whole race of beings, the Dineen, whom we knew to be here at that time."

"I've studied some of the writings of that cataclysm period," Eila said. "Almost all of the intelligent mass of the Earth and its sister planets was degraded into chemical, magnetic, and heat energy. Any seeds for regeneration of life would have had to have been hidden in stony wastes, or in the vapors left streaming above the ruined planets."

"Exactly," Drost said. "But the rude concepts of life entertained by Earth's scientists now recognize only an evolution that has occurred after the great explosion. They do not realize they themselves have mutated from a prior consciousness already existing before that historic explosion they call The Big Bang of Creation."

"It doesn't seem the present humans are as avaricious and warlike as the old Dineen we've studied about, nor as intelligent. Our historians say the Dineen conquered and subjected all of their sister planets." Eila said.

"And the creature standing there has all the reborn consciousness of a purebred, ancient Dineen warrior," Drost said.

Eila looked distastefully at the creature. "How was it accomplished?"

Drost laughed. "Do you remember my geomagnetic measurements of the rock sample from the Nevada mountain? The data showed it dated from the Corso explosion. Afterward, my bio-intelligence experiments yielded an extraordinary response, proving an entombed presence of the Dineen. I've used that rock sample as the nucleus of this, my lovely Macnessa. The former lords of the Universe have been reborn here as the animus of an ugly fungus, modeled after the Macnessa phalluspod of our own planet, a symbol of ripe, universal fertility."

"Won't the Dineen consciousness rebel against what you've done? It seems such a grotesque marriage of their own seed with the Macnessa," Eila said.

"Yes, an exquisite union. However, though I've made the

noble Dineen a prisoner of its new carriage, I've given it hope. It can hope to overcome its fetid, corporal being with time, and perhaps evolve back into its former greatness and beauty. However, it can just as well fear that I may destroy it and send it hurtling back into the limbo of frozen consciousness where I found it, a rock in the crust of a declining planet."

The Macnessa remained immobile on the platform and watched them with its baleful, half-shuttered orb.

"If this creature is going to be around us maybe you'd better arm me with one of your weapons."

"Yes, take this one. It's a heat-sink ray that can sap all heat energy and consciousness in its path. At full intensity it can slow all molecular activity in any organism. Every molecule implodes inward toward becoming an inert, rock-like mass. At full intensity I could have reduced our Macnessa back into the fungus-covered rock from which it sprang. Even now, I shall have to use the magnascan to revitalize the creature."

Eila examined the weapon and cradled it against folded arms. "Why did you take such elaborate means to detect unfaithful slags?" she said.

"The mysteries of the Macnessa will hold a certain supernatural terror for our slags. The fear of being discovered and swallowed up by the Macnessa should help dissuade any who might be tempted to wander from the path of orthodoxy. They will be taught how the Macnessa can search out and detect the unfaithful.."

Eila coughed and turned her head away from the fumes

rising off the Macnessa. "And how is this creature able to detect such sinners?

"Its core being was so polarized by the Corso cataclysm that it responds to infinitely small aberrations in electromagnetic fields. It can easily sense small misalignments in beryllium strands that should occur in unfaithful slags."

The Macnessa showed signs of movement and Eila unfolded her arms and brought the heat-sink gun to her side. "What happens when it detects them?"

Drost laughed. "It's been commanded to devour the apostate." He eyed the slowly palpitating, wind-sucking Macnessa, and loosed another throaty laugh. "If it serves us well, I will see that it enjoys a further chance to climb from the numb matter of earth to a more noble self-sustained being."

"I will not fail you," the Macnessa said, its wheezing voice issuing through the hair-covered slit below its orb.

"The creature speaks again," Eila said. "Could it have damaged you if you had not subdued it with your weapon?"

"Perhaps. Its tactic would be to try swallowing me whole, leach out my organic interior, and excrete my beryllium carcass." Drost laughed and opened his arms as if he would embrace the Macnessa. The creature tilted its head and backed away. Drost wiped spittle from his mouth with the back of his hand and stifled his laughter. "No, never trust it, my dear, but do not fear it. It must learn that the Skatha are its masters."

Outside the window, Vasthi nudged Josiah and whispered, "We've seen and heard enough." She removed the listening apparatus from the pane. "Let's get back down the wall."

"I'm ready," he said. "But we've got to get you off this island before they try to test you with that creature."

"I'm not leaving before I have the secret of the slagging technology from Eila," she said. "I need to void any remaining hold he might have on my willpower, and I want to be able to use the benefits of that technology for future slags. They can help me do a lot of good in the world."

Josiah looked at her with skepticism. "With you programmed as their leader, I suppose?"

"Why not?" she said and laughed.

He thought about that and marveled how they'd managed to stay together this long.

CHAPTER 13—Mission Plan

Vasthi blew on her hands as she waited outside the window to Eila's quarters and watched. More than two hours had passed since she'd left Josiah. She glanced up at the moon, her watch, and back to the window.

Inside, Eila rested her head in folded arms on the table. A small, enameled box lay open on the tabletop, with a silver spoon and two lacquered wood chips beside it, one bare, the other heaped with a white powder. A candle set in a holder on the stone wall flickered in a draft of air. Shadows of objects danced on the bleached wood tabletop[.

Vasthi opened her shoulder bag and rummaged until she found a small folded paper. She removed her wristwatch and laid it on the window ledge. Opening a small compartment in the clasp assembly and cupping her hand to shield it from the wind, she tapped powder from the paper into the watch compartment. She put the watch back on, tugged her army field jacket straight, and walked from the small garden area to the heavy, plank door. Taking a quick, deep breath, she knocked. After a long wait with no answer she knocked again. This time she heard a chair slide and slow, irregular steps approached. The door opened and Eila stared at her. Her speech was slow and halting.

"You—what is it you want?"

"Only to speak with you. Just two days remain for our stay on the island and we may not see each other again for a long while. May I come in?" she said.

Eila hesitated. "Perhaps it would be better if we talked another time. I've succumbed this night into a dark, despairing mood and I—"

Vasthi stepped inside and put her arm about Eila's waist. "There are times when one needs a friend," Vasthi said. "I'm sure if I had no one but Drost to talk with day in and day out I would be quite despairing also."

Eila allowed herself to be guided back to her seat at the table. Vasthi drew up another chair and sat near her. She studied Eila's face for a moment and reached out to run her fingers through her flowing silver hair. She leaned and kissed Eila on the lips. Eila stiffened and drew back. She tried to speak several times, but could not. Vasthi ran her hand over Eila's body, touching, questioning, and Eila seemed awed.

"I do not wear a human sheath, never have, and my tactile sense is at a very low level. Yet, you've made me tremble. I've never before felt such emotional tension, but then such conduct between women has been dealt with severely for centuries on Aquama, beginning when our race was threatened with extinction."

Vasthi smiled. "There are no such constraints here," she said. "We shall explore our sensuality further," and she leaned forward to force her tongue past Eila's lips. Vasthi went almost as rigid as Eila when she made contact. Eila's tongue startled her with its un-textured, silken warmth that moved and flowed with a curious surface tension on her own. Vasthi's heart pounded and she sought to turn her fear into design as she lingered for some moments. Stray currents of their unequal bioelectric forces ebbed and flowed between them. Vasthi broke off the embrace and sat shaken and breathless for several minutes while an amused Eila looked at her.

Vasthi managed a smile and nodded to the lacquered chip heaped with powder. "What is it?" she asked.

Eila looked vacantly at the things on the table and dismissed them with a wave of her hand. "Cocaine, my means of a brief escape from the longing to share more fully your human condition. Instead of some infinite sense of superiority that Drost enjoys, I feel a sense of deep yearning."

Vasthi was surprised to discover that the jewel-woman could weep. The candlelight refracted with opalescent fire in streaks of moisture coursing down her aquamarine visage.

"What are your feelings toward Josiah?" Vasthi asked.

Eila stared at her, not speaking. Vasthi grew uncomfortable and looked toward the cocaine. "Do you mind if I try some?" she said.

"Please, help yourself," Eila said, "though I'd caution you about its strange effects."

"I've tried it before," she said, taking up the chip in her hand. She took a pinch and sniffed deeply, then laid the chip back on the table. She stretched clasped hands out, tilted her head back and moaned. A quick squeeze of a palm against the watchband and a powder emptied unseen over the cocaine chip. She smiled and moved the chip in front of Eila. After staring at it a moment, Eila took a pinch, inhaled deeply, and leaned back in her chair. Vasthi clasped and unclasped her hands, glancing between the sweeping second hand of her watch and Eila.

"Eila," she said, finally, "see whether you can repeat after me, please—one, two… and she waited for a response. Eila seemed confused, tried to speak, and responded haltingly up to two.

"Three…four," Vasthi continued. Eila gave back the numbers as if an automaton. Vasthi smiled and touched her arm, "Listen carefully to me. I wish to learn the secrets of the materials and technology for creating and designing slags. Do you understand?" she said.

"Yes, I understand," Eila said, her voice wispy and soft. She groped for lost words, and said finally, "I'm traveling to Tupa Inca tonight to pick up slagging materials that should be ready by now." She lost her thoughts for a moment. "I can take you with me and show you what you'd like to learn," she said, her voice coming slow and lethargic.

"How would we get there?" Vasthi said.

"Our reconnaissance craft—Griffin—in the powerboat shed. The cove."

"Good. Is it safe to leave now—what about Drost?"

"He's probably drunk himself into a stupor by now. Been drinking heavily the past year. We must leave soon."

"Good," Vasthi said, rising to take Eila by the hand. "Let's go, my exotic one; we have much to accomplish before this night is through. But before we leave, where is the heat-sink gun that Drost gave you?"

"The gun? It—it's in a drawer of that desk. How did you know of it?"

116

"That's not important, but we'll take it with us." She went over to the desk, opened drawers, and found the gun. She mimicked Drost's moves, located the intensity slide, examined it, and tested the heft of the gun in her hand.

The two women left the apartment and walked to the beach. The wind was cold and wet and the smell of shellfish and kelp hung in the air. They followed along the stony beach to a long, dilapidated hulk of a building, supported by slender timber piles marching out into sheltered cove waters. Eila led the way onto the wood catwalk running along the side, and they entered the shed through a doorway. The tide had dropped and the Griffin rocked low in the water between the piers. Eila withdrew her small command module from a pocket. Vasthi had her explain the module functions to her before Eila used it to open the hatch door. They climbed down a ladder, crossed a gangway, and stepped onto the craft. Inside, Eila coupled the command module to the large, on-board computer and entered her flight programming.

Her voice remained hollow but more certain. "Strap yourself into that chair," she said, as she buckled herself into the commander's chair. "I'll launch under manual control and switch to computer after we're aloft."

Vasthi eased into the second officer's chair and strapped herself in. She watched Eila, who continued staring ahead at a blackened panel.

"Are you all right?" Vasthi said.

Eila straightened in her chair, "Of course," she said. She pressed a button on the control panel and the cockpit window shields lifted. The rows of piles on either side of the narrow passage ahead seemed to swing back and forth as the Griffin rocked in the water. She activated the drive and a faintly throbbing hum filled the cockpit. A blue glow lit the piles and shed walls ahead of them. Abruptly, she pulled back the controls and the Griffin leaped forward. Waves slapped violently at the hull and the rows of piles danced up and down. A sudden, splintering pop as they sideswiped a pile, a lurching side to side motion as Eila fought chattering hand controls to damp the violent deflections, and they cleared the shed to soar into the air.

CHAPTER 14—Editing Slags

Vasthi rubbed at her temple. Letting Eila drive under the influence with a mind-control drug on top of cocaine was obviously risky. "What happened back there?" Vasthi said.

Eila banked the Griffin and looked down toward the shed. The last half was splintered and squatted lower in the water. "I don't know what is the matter with me," she said. The cocaine never dulled my senses like this before." She put the Griffin into a climb and continued toward the mainland.

"Maybe you'd better give me a few pointers on maneuvering this ship in case you don't feel up to landing it," Vasthi said.

"When we approach Tupa Inca the land-based computer will take over for automatic landing," Eila said, "but if you wish, I can give you a chance at the manual controls. You've had flight training?"

"Yes, I'm qualified in some of the latest jet fighter aircraft."

"Marvelous," Eila said, her voice too dull to be ironic. "You'll probably have no difficulty then." She took the craft off automatic pilot and spent time during the flight to familiarize Vasthi with the controls and handling of the craft. Vasthi was elated with the smooth responses and extraordinary maneuverability of the Griffin and could have spent hours at it, but more important matters were at hand.

"We have so much to try to accomplish tonight that we'd better get on with it," Vasthi said.

"Accomplish? Yes, you're right; there are things we meant to accomplish."

They approached within miles of the mainland, rising steeply to avoid commercial air lanes, and soared over the coastal plains high above the Andes. Descending in altitude, the Griffin followed a narrow, silvery ribbon of water tracing a path through the mountains.

Eila pointed through the cabin window. "There, on the ridge ahead—Tupa Inca."

A low beeping signal sounded as Vasthi peered out at the moonlit ridge. A green light flashed on the control panel as the incoming guidance system took command of the Griffin and moved it along a tightly descending spiral to the ridge top. The craft abruptly decelerated, hovered a moment above the ground while the stone platform slid open, and quickly sank into the holding bay. Lights in the bay came on as the overhead platform closed.

"Welcome to Tupa Inca," Eila said, gesturing with uplifted hands, and she unbuckled from her chair. She uncoupled the portable control module from the onboard computer, actuated it, and the door of the Griffin slid open.

"Let's go immediately to Drost's laboratory," Vasthi said.

Eila led the way along tunnel corridors and they stopped outside the laboratory. Vasthi peered through the window into the lighted room. It was unoccupied and they entered and went to an equipment-filled workbench.

"As soon as Drost receives all of the processed beryllium from Josiah, he'll prepare our remaining fifty-thousand strands and catalyst he needs to complete his organization

120

of slags," Eila said. "He has only about five-thousand doses of finished preparation here, and some of these will be distributed at the end of this conference—to those slags who survive the Night of the Macnessa. They'll take our remaining doses with them to their home temples and recruit additional slags for the Inca Foundation."

"Not much time left," Vasthi said. "Let's begin. Suppose you lead me through the production steps for the strands and catalyst, tell me what you know about each stage, and I'll ask questions as we go."

In halting, sometimes disconnected logic, Eila covered the various stages of preparing and programming the beryllium strands and formulating the catalyst. Vasthi's new internal, slag intelligence was often sufficient to bridge gaps in the instructions, or to elicit missing and needed information from Eila. In addition, she took time to download data from the production computers onto several miniature nano-optic memory drives she'd brought with her. By the time she replaced the drives in her bag, they had enough to equal the volume of data in the advanced military research library of her own country. For several hours they walked about in the laboratory, discussing the functional role of the equipment and trying it out on samples of strands and catalyst. During this time Eila became more agitated as her system fought off the effects of the drug. Vasthi noticed it and hurried her along.

"The machine you called the strand programming editor," Vasthi said. "That's one I'm particularly interested in; tell me about that again and in more detail."

Eila sat on the edge of the workbench and switched on the editor. She watched the flashing display screen and gave oral commands to skip through an index of sub-routines in the program. She said, "Drost developed this editor in a pragmatic, trial-and-error way. In early experiments, he used various philosophical and political science precepts in his program that occasionally fell into disfavor with him later on. Imagine if he'd input a vast amount of published learning into the program and then foolishly loaded it with the ethics of an ordinary general before discovering someone like Genghis Khan. He designed this machine and wrote his program so that it could rapidly superimpose new ethics and guideline derivatives onto an earlier database and its already prepared strands and catalyst. In that way his latest heroes could be given the greatest weighting in a slag's reasoning power."

Vasthi was pleased. "Yes, I like that possibility of imposing a new type of leadership and directions without losing a huge original database."

Eila folded her arms across her chest and smiled. "But that's only a possibility for programming new slags, Vasthi, not existing slags."

Vasthi chewed at her lip, and her eyes lost some of their luster. "Yes, for the moment. But at least one of his present slags may be strong enough to continue overriding her program."

"You? Perhaps. And those who are not so strong?"

"They'll have to be—overwritten—somehow, or maybe discarded."

Eila's peals of laughter unsettled Vasthi; perhaps the effects of the drug on Eila were fading. She took a flask from her jacket and emptied the contents of another packet into it.

"You've become overly tired," she said, offering the flask to Eila. "This should refresh you."

Eila remained with arms folded.

"Do as I say," Vasthi ordered. "Drink this, now."

Eila took the small flask, put it to her lips, and swallowed. She laid the flask aside and sat straight on the workbench.

"What a strange creature," Vasthi whispered. "I've probably given you enough to knock down an elephant and you just sit there." She watched Eila for a few moments, and then set about her task. Moving quickly, she gathered the trays of finished strands and catalyst from the magnetic resonance machine. A tray held nine hundred capsules, each no larger than the tip of a small finger. She stacked trays on the workbench next to the editing machine, sat at the keyboard, and crunched the stiffness from her fingers. Not enough time to be too sophisticated; the philosophical and ethical constructs of the slag's reasoning could be left as is but they would have to recognize her as their leader. Basically, she'd only need to input operators and control functions to the slagging program, so that all Drost identities became Vasthi identities. A bit egocentric and draconian? Perhaps, but it would have to suffice.

She wrote out her equations in longhand using the programming language identified by Eila, input them into the machine, tested the program response to several calibrated constructions of war-or-peace diplomatic problems and to several life-or-death situations. She adjusted her programming until the outcomes were roughly suitable to her strategies.

Hours later, a third notebook had almost been filled with equations and after she'd entered the last of them she closed her notebook and got up from the computer, running her fingers through her hair and showing her exhaustion in deep breathing.

"Why do you do this…are you no better than Drost?" Eila said, standing nearby holding to a tabletop, her voice halting and slurred.

Vasthi tossed her hands up, "Yes, what drives me so?" she said, plaintively. "Did I go mad when my family was blown up by a suicide bomber or has this torment and cold emotion always lived within me? Have I been mad from then, or from birth? Or am I not mad at all but only born to subdue those fanatics who would scourge this earth?"

"But you have no qualms about using Drost's methods to accomplish your goals?"

"What does it matter if I have to usurp the flabby freewill of five thousand aimless people? The world will profit from it. My disciples will serve me well to help destroy the fanatics and devils of this world whoever they may be." She thrust one of the trays of capsules into Eila's hands. "Begin—we'll run the capsules through the machine."

An hour later they were finished and the materials were stowed on board the Griffin along with the refined beryllium Drost needed. Eila had grown increasingly lethargic and when she had strapped herself into the command seat, she slumped forward. Vasthi pulled her upright and revived her with an inhaler.

"Just a while longer my lovely jewel woman; I shall need

124

you just a while longer," Vasthi said. "If you're not feeling up to it, I think I've learned enough of your craft to get us back to the island but I will need you to launch from this subterranean vault."

"I'm all right," Eila said, but she shook her head and grimaced. "Or maybe not so all right. Perhaps if I could rest for a while?"

"There's really no time; we've got to get back to the island. It's almost dawn and I don't want us to be missed by Drost. He mustn't know I was with you tonight. I don't want him to suspect anything until I'm ready for him."

Eila took a deep breath, checked the coupling of the control module to the on-board computer, and punched in the launch and navigation coding. She waited till the gage needle rose to full power and glanced to Vasthi.

"Ready?" she said.

Vasthi nodded and Eila tapped the launch button. The stone roof slid back, the Griffin's engines hummed, and seconds later the craft soared into the night sky. A veil of pre-dawn light spread over the dark ridges and peaks of the Andes as they sped westward. A carpet of pin-point lights revealed the city of Quito nestled into a broad valley, then blankets of clouds lay below as they approached the coast, and minutes later they flashed out over the ocean.

As soon as the islands were in sight, Vasthi rose from her chair. She unbuckled Eila and lifted her by the arm to her feet. Eila was confused but followed her to the hatch door.

"Stand there a moment," Vasthi said.

"Why—what is it you want me to do?"

"Don't be so querulous. I'll show you in due time." Vasthi returned to the controls and strapped herself in at the command seat. She scanned the controls, took the craft off automatic pilot, and tested the response. Satisfied, she turned toward Eila, activated a control button, and the hatch door slid open behind Eila. The wind tore at her long hair whipping it across her face so that only her glowing eyes penetrated the silvery veil.

"You would destroy me," Eila cried out.

"Vasthi took the heat-sink gun from her bag, aimed it, and fired. Eila fell backward out of the hatchway. Vasthi banked the Griffin sharply and brought it back over the area, sweeping low over the sea with the Griffin's blue-hued searchlights skimming the waves. She made several passes until she felt confident that the sea had swallowed Eila. Breaking away, she continued on to her destination. Before she arrived, a faint glow of yellow and rose sky marked the horizon beyond the island. With the shed ruined, she made a beach landing in a small cove farther down the shoreline. She carried the carton of capsules from the craft and closed the hatchway. Another control button activated the Griffin's surface LED panels which superimposed the colors and shapes of the surrounding rocks and sand terrain on the craft, obscuring it from view.

CHAPTER 15—Tower Strike

The sun had already climbed above the horizon when Vasthi entered the compound. A cool breeze swept in from the sea and she hugged the carton of capsules to her chest. Hurrying to the east wing where the conference-goers were quartered she entered and went quickly down a hallway. She paused outside Josiah's door, looked both ways, and checked the doorknob. It was unlocked and she went inside. Pausing to accustom her eyes to the dark interior, she made out a wooden bench, writing table, and bedroom door. She went to the door and opened it.

"Josiah," she called softly. The mattress creaked as he turned, silence for a few moments, and he bolted upright.

"Who is it?"

"Vasthi," she said. She set the carton down, rushed to throw her arms around him as he rose from the bed, and pressed her face against his chest. She stood back, gripped the neckline of his pajama shirt, and ripped it open. Buttons clattered to the floor and she pressed her face to his chest, twisting it from side to side.

"What is it, what's happened?" he said.

She said nothing but her breathing was agitated and her heart pounded. Gradually she calmed but avoided looking at him while she spoke.

"I went with Eila to Tupa Inca to get some of the slagging materials. I had to—I had to destroy her. You understand that, don't you? I had to destroy her. She's too loyal to Drost and we couldn't have trusted her."

He let out a groan and was unable to speak.

"I had to, don't you understand? I had to," she kept insisting. Josiah remained silent. "She meant something to you after all, didn't she?" Vasthi said. "Please say something. I didn't want to do it, but she's not even human. She doesn't have any real feelings for you or any other human. She's not a real person, not a real person at all, just a bio-metallic alien from another world. Akla ordered you to destroy the beryllium eaters, didn't she?"

"But I argued with her to spare Eila. I'm not going to judge you for what you thought you had to do," he said. "I'm devastated by what happened, but we've got to go on. You're as confused as I am about this whole thing—but you were wrong about Eila. She was a real person, very real." He squeezed his eyes closed and shook his head. "What do we do now?" he said.

"No one is safe until we've destroyed Drost and his abomination, the Macnessa. We need to do it now."

He gritted his teeth and frowned. "How?"

"With the heat-sink gun I took from Eila."

Minutes later, they made their way across the dust-blown compound to the north wing where the Skatha were quartered. They huddled together in a recessed doorway of a connecting corridor between the apartments and the stone tower.

"Locked," Josiah said, tugging at the knob.

128

"Stand away," Vasthi said, and she drew a small, plastic container from her pack. Fine streams of liquid spurted from the container onto the brass doorknob, where it boiled and smoked. Seconds later, the remains of the knob dropped to the floor. She pushed the tip of the container against the smoking shaft and the far half of the knob fell to the floor inside the room. They pressed their ears to the door, listening, but no sounds followed other than the turbulent shearing of wind over the stone buildings. They pushed open the door, slipped inside, and wedged it shut behind them. Hurrying toward the apartments, they stopped at the first doorway.

"The room layout showed Drost closest to the tower so this should be it," she whispered.

"I don't hear anything inside," he said. "We might be lucky and surprise him while he's still asleep. It's locked, though—give me the acid and get ready with that gun."

She handed him the acid container and drew the heat-sink gun from her pack. Josiah burned through, caught the knob in his handkerchief, and laid it aside. A quick push on the shaft and the rest of the lockset clattered to the floor inside. Vasthi pushed against the door with her back and spun inside, her gun held in outstretched hands. She swept the room, head and gun darting to each shadowy form. No one, nothing moved, empty. Papers lay scattered over the writing table and floor, clothes were heaped on the couch, and two locker chests were stacked in a corner of the room.

"What a stink," Josiah said. "The Macnessa?"

"Don't know—the bedroom door, open it," she said, gun at the ready.

He rushed over and tried the knob. It gave and he kicked open the door. She ran past him, dropped to a kneeling position inside and panned the room with her gun barrel—an empty disheveled bed, blinds rattling in the breeze through an open window, a shirt draped on the back of a chair. He'd been there the night before, but he was gone now. She let out an explosive breath and sank onto a crouch.

"We'll have to try the tower," she said.

"At least we won't have to go up that wall again," he said. "And we've got a heat-sink gun even if Drost and the Macnessa are up there waiting for us."

She rose slowly to her feet. Her face showed the strain of her long night's work. "Let's go," she said.

They hurried from the room, ran down the corridor, and took the steps two-at-a-time up the spiraling stairwell of the tower. Slowing near the top, they crept up the remaining steps. The door to the lookout room was ajar. Drafts of air seeped through outer walls and around window frames and pushed against the swinging, spring-loaded door. They flattened against the wall and Josiah used his foot to open the door wider. They listened, Vasthi poised with the gun and waiting.

"Let me have that," he said. "I'll go in first this time." She shook her head, swept around him into the room and spun in all directions, jerking the muzzle from one fluttering sound to another. After a few seconds she lowered the gun. She bit at her lip and her eyes glazed with tears of frustration. Josiah came up beside her.

"He's evading us," he said. "He must have something

special in mind."

"Perhaps—look, the doorway to the outside."

It opened slowly at first, before a stiff, gusting wind sent it crashing against the inner wall. Vasthi's nostrils quivered and her eyes grew wide. Josiah recoiled and covered his nose and mouth with his hand. The Macnessa moved through the doorway and a stench billowed across the room. A slug-like secretion spread outward from the writhing tentacles of its footpad and the phallic stump glided over the slickened stone threshold and into the room. The door banged repeatedly against the wall as the wind blew. The domed head twisted to train its black orb on each of them.

"I am the Macnessa, but do not fear me. I sense that one in this room has the noble powers of a slag, but one weakened by an internal conflict. Trust me, child. Speak to me and I will help you."

"Help? —Yes, you would help, you filthy beast," Vasthi said. "You mean only to destroy me." She trembled and drew rapid, quick breaths. Josiah circled to the side, momentarily drawing the Macnessa's attention away from Vasthi who stood frozen with gun in hand. The Macnessa darted Josiah a quick look and turned back to Vasthi.

"Calm yourself, my pretty," it said, as it advanced toward her with sucking sounds. "Come, touch me with your hands and taste of my spores and you shall become as great and powerful as the Skatha. My spores secrete the essence of immortal life and great power."

Josiah shouted, "Shoot it, Vasthi, shoot."

She struggled to steady the heat-sink gun. The

131

Macnessa's black orb bulged from its socket and the orifices over its body pumped and wheezed, filling the air with the cloying stench of sewer gas. A magnetic field emanated from the Macnessa and created an irresistible pull on the bio-metallic compound within Vasthi, drawing her forward. The air between them became highly charged and ionized into a sparking cloud.

"Josiah," screamed Vasthi. "It controls me—take the gun."

The Macnessa lurched sideways to intercept Josiah. Its tentacles thrashed wildly to propel it forward. The ponderous, leathery head yawed and pitched as it bore ahead, its pumping orifices wheezing and sucking gulps of air. The Macnessa's charge came too slow, and Josiah got around it to reach Vasthi's side. He wrested the gun from her stiffened hand and aimed it as the Macnessa wheeled to face them.

"Wait, Josiah, wait," it moaned. The voice came on wheezing puffs of air through the hair covered slit. "You know not what you do. In time, I will deal with the Skatha and I will remember you for what mercy you showed me. Once, this beast you see before you was a member of the most noble warrior race in the Original One's creation. If you spare me and let me conquer Drost, the evil that has befallen us can be undone, and your own race will profit magnificently."

"No, you can freeze up for a few thousand more millennia," Josiah said. "You won't ever recover from what you are now to what you once were. What Drost gave you was only a corrupted and ugly start on any path back to an evolved consciousness. Both of you are aberrations that need to be destroyed."

132

"No, don't be foolish. Drost is a powerful force and you need me to help subdue him," the Macnessa protested, showing a resumption of its rage. The black orb strained in its socket and the orifices pumped furiously open and shut. "What is the loss of this artificially-intelligent woman to you? Stay your hand and let me destroy her and the other slags. Be my secret ally until I overcome Drost and have him do our bidding. You will be rewarded beyond your greatest dreams."

While the Macnessa held Josiah's attention, it had crept forward. Now, with a screech and a flailing of tentacles, it flew at him. Josiah shoved Vasthi to the side and activated the gun. The Macnessa gasped as the freezing beam stabbed deep, but its rush carried it onto Josiah. He choked in its fumes and cried out as the Macnessa pulled his leg into a gulping orifice. Dozens of writhing, saw-toothed tongues lacerated his leg, and digestive juices melted into his flesh. The Macnessa's weight flattened the gun against Josiah's chest, preventing its use. Tentacles tugged at Josiah's free arm, drawing it toward another orifice. He screamed and butted his head violently into the glaring orb. The Macnessa shrieked and faltered, enough for Josiah to free his gun from beneath its weight. He rammed the barrel of the gun deep into the gelatinous orb and activated.

The Macnessa howled in pain and terror. It choked on its cries and slumped away. Josiah kept the gun buried in the orb and struggled to pull free from under the Macnessa's weight. He yanked what was left of his lacerated, shriveled leg from the orifice and held his aim on the stiffening, screaming head with the gun on full activation. The last vestiges of life faded from what now resembled a pockmarked boulder covered with beautiful red and brown-colored lichen. Josiah dragged himself clear of the inert mass, shaking and breathing heavily.

Vasthi lifted him with his arm around her shoulder, "Hold onto me," she said. "I'll get you outside. We need to get you some help. Can you put some weight on your good leg?"

"Grab that cloth from the table first and let's bandage what's left of my leg."

She sat him on a chair and knotted the cloth around his thigh to stem the bleeding and wrapped the rest of the cloth around the residue of his lower leg and foot.

"I think I'm going to be sick," she said. "It almost had you."

"Every once in a while I win one."

She gave a white-faced smile and helped him outside, where he leaned against the tower railing. He pointed to a tiny figure near the rim of a distant cove along the shore. Vasthi leaned over the railing and stared at where he pointed.

"That's about where I left the Griffin," Vasthi said. "Drost might have become aware by now that Eila was missing and he's located the Griffin with his command module."

"Can we go after him and finish this thing," he said.

She looked dubiously from his leg to his contorted face. "You can't go anywhere until you have that leg taken care of. I'll radio my ship to report a failed terrorist attack and get some assistance. We'll have some medical help for you on board—I'll tell them you were wounded stepping on an IED."

Josiah nodded and passed out.

The next day, Josiah woke to find himself in the recovery room of the ship's sick bay. They had amputated his leg below the knee. The nurse saw him stir and hurried off to telephone Vasthi. While he waited for her, he pulled together the bits and pieces of the previous day's events. Vasthi arrived at the sick bay soon after.

"I hope the Galactic Druids have good medical insurance and a retirement plan for amputee Druids," he said. "What happened with Drost?"

"Gone," she said, laying a hand on his shoulder. "As soon as the landing party arrived we headed up the beach to the cove. When I saw the Griffin was gone I kept things simple and just let them continue the search for a terrorist of Drost's description."

"So he's still around," Josiah said. "What good am I going to be to you now with me on crutches."

Vasthi sank into a chair next to the bed and covered her eyes. "We're going to have you fitted with a prosthesis, Josiah. But you've done enough; you can leave the rest to me."

"No way," he said. "He's ruined my life but somehow I'll still finish him."

CHAPTER 16—Temple

Josiah spent another two weeks on the ship recuperating. Vasthi sat with him on deck for hours each day, talking of her plans for a takeover of the Inca Foundation and the directions she would go with it to make the world a better place. Josiah remained wary of such grandiose plans and tried to convince her they should simply take his share of money from the beryllium sale and find a life in Ecuador.

"What about Drost and your mission to destroy him?" she asked.

"Yes, that's still a problem and one where I'd probably need your help."

"It's so critical now to get the Inca Foundation up and running," she said, "and I've got to see to that. I know, it's also important to put an end to Drost, but we need to do that as discreetly as possible. It wouldn't be good for the Foundation if we brought any attention to what went on at Tupa Inca. The slagging research is best left mysterious. Give me time to arrange the cooperation of a few officials and to organize a Special Forces team and we'll take care of both problems simultaneously at Tupa Inca. If Drost becomes a threat to you before then, we'll deal with him."

Josiah reached beside the deck chair and picked up his beer. "When will we see each other again after this?"

"Every month or two. Before another year goes by everything will be in place—can we go with that?"

Josiah drank his beer and leaned back in the chair. It might give him the time he needed to think things through. She was a remarkable, awesome woman, but her huge ambitions troubled him. He clicked his glass with hers.

A month later, Josiah waited in anticipation as he felt the aura take hold. He'd fasted for three days and with his prosthesis was able to walk long distances outside his residence in Quito, purposely driving himself to exhaustion each day, and now the aura he sought had returned.

Akla waited, seated on a stone wall near the edge of a cliff. The thunderous break of the sea far below shook the ground surface, and the raucous calls of seagulls punctuated the dull roar. Josiah squinted his eyes—trying to make her out through the mist.

He approached closer. "I had to speak with you again," he said. "I missed another attempt to destroy Drost and was almost swallowed up by a monster he'd created instead. Lost a leg in that dazzling episode. Things are getting pretty desperate—I need your advice." He waited for her to speak.

"I'm sorry about your amputated leg. Go on," Akla said.

Her lackluster tone troubled him. He'd grown used to hearing the fire and mockery in her voice. "Do you know all of what else has happened? Drost has ordered Eila to slag some important people around the world. They've been programmed to be geniuses that act according to Drost's will. Then Vasthi destroyed Eila—which absolutely stunned me—and now she thinks she can transfer the slags loyalty to herself. She's even prepared to create more of her own

138

slags. She's some sort of idealist, wants to defeat terrorists and fanatics everywhere, and thinks she can lead an organization of powerful, super-intelligent people that will benefit the world."

"But they'll be slags, nonetheless—only Vasthi's slags." Akla said, her voice rising to be heard above the roar of the sea.

He said, "What's the difference whether such people are taught for twenty years at the best universities, or they swallow their knowledge in a cocktail glass?"

The same rasping voice spoke, "All true learning passes into universal consciousness and lasts forever; knowledge bestowed without building on such universal learning will vanish with the holder."

Akla stood now, resting a hand on the hilt of her sword and peering over the rim of her tall battle shield toward the horizon. Josiah was perplexed. She wasn't exactly cheering him on to join forces with Vasthi.

"Okay, she's programmed herself as their leader but she's not evil," he said. "She's a strong leader and might help bring justice to a world in danger of self-destructing."

The warrior woman walked to the edge of the cliff and looked back over her shield at Josiah. "You must go on!" Her laughter rose above the din of the sea and she was gone.

Vasthi's frantic schedule allowed only a weekend getaway with Josiah in the following months. He took a leave from his job at the powerhouse and searched for land he might be able to buy in several high valleys southeast of the site. A small, barely surviving rancho in the district of Quecha caught his eye; he managed to purchase it and set to work installing an improved irrigation system before returning to his job at the powerhouse. He'd only been back a few days when another worker disappeared from the work camp, the second, he learned, in the past four months. Still, workers did quit occasionally to simply return to their villages. He would have liked to visit Kepo to learn if there'd been any sightings of Drost, or any activity at Tupa Inca, but he feared venturing anywhere outside the camp. In his calls to Vasthi he pressed to know when her plans to strike Tupa Inca would be ready. She begged him to be patient, the plan required the discrete complicity of a number of officials. Meanwhile Josiah agonized, and suffered another seizure. In the accompanying aura, Akla ridiculed his lack of determination in confronting Drost.

"Perhaps it's as well to remove you from this assignment now," she said, sitting beside a campfire and fingering the knots along a length of deer sinew hanging from her belt.

"That would probably suit me," Josiah said. "I'm already one leg short."

"You don't understand. If you're removed. or I arrive at the last knot on this war thong and you haven't yet destroyed Drost, your time on earth shall be up," she said.

Josiah blanched. "In that case, I'd rather stay on and maybe I can do better." He held his hands to his ears to shut out her laughter as he spiraled through the star-filled blackness and back toward consciousness.

Several months later, a chauffeured limousine pulled alongside a pier on an idle, decaying stretch of the San Francisco waterfront. A spacious, post-modern building, newly refurbished from an aging warehouse, stood at the entrance to the pier. The first floor took up half the width of the pier; the next two stories diminished in width, in pyramid fashion up to a penthouse block at the pinnacle.

Vasthi and Josiah emerged from the limousine. Near the entrance to the building two men dressed in long, multi-hued woolen ponchos intercepted them. When they recognized Vasthi they bowed and stepped aside to allow her and Josiah to enter the building. Inside, the smell of incense perfumed the air. Stained glass windows set high in the walls picked up the soft interior lighting with strong, vibrant, earth colors. Their footsteps echoed from the polished hardwood floor as they walked to a ceremony in progress at the far end of the room.

About thirty people in white gowns sat cross-legged on the floor, bent forward with foreheads touching the floor and arms outstretched, chanting a low, cadenced mantra. Vasthi and Josiah stopped at the edge of the group and looked across toward a darkened stage area. The sound of a muted drum came from behind the stage backdrop curtain, and a staccato beat quickened in tempo and intensity. A man rose from the stage floor and slowly unwound to full height as colored shafts of light lit the stage from overhead. His arms stretched wide to open a black cloak and expose a gold sunburst medallion secured by leather thongs across his bare chest. Those on the floor rose to erect sitting positions and joined in a rhythmic clapping. The man on stage began a choreography of ballet-like movements, keeping the sunburst hidden for periods, then baring it to an accompaniment of frenzied drumming, flute music, and chanting voices.

Vasthi and Josiah turned and walked to an elevator shaft at the center of the room. Vasthi used her key to open the door and punched the control panel for the top floor. They remained silent as the elevator rose but Josiah's frown and tight lips showed his uneasiness.

"All these rituals have me jumpy," he said, as they left the elevator. "Who made up that production?"

"Such rituals and symbolism are needed when you're trying to build the dedication of followers for a hard job ahead. I thought it was rather artful; several university students collaborated. It's quite in keeping with what people really want. Modernism has tried to purge life of so much of its treasured mystical and ritual content and to substitute instead doses of scientism, rationalism, and ultimately, atheism. Cultural leaders forget that most people are not that far removed from primitive peasant stock. They may have adapted superficially to the changing cultural environment, but their psyches still lie close to their peasant mores."

"But you're a different sort of leader—a well intentioned aristocrat."

"Yes, you could say that," Vasthi said, stung by his remark. "It is foolish to pretend there is no need for an aristocracy. Perhaps it's not fashionable to say so, but an aristocratic class is necessary to the proper functioning of society. The so-called middle class, or your bourgeois, is merely a pretentious element of the peasant class. A destabilizing force occurs when an evil aristocracy exploits

142

the brutish nature of peasants and enslaves them. Our alien Skatha would make himself the head of such an aristocracy, but I won't let that happen."

"The sort of power you're after will be resented by some people. It won't come easily."

"People may be loathe to acknowledge it, but their lives have always seen greater security and harmony when living under the rule of compassionate autocrats."

"Is that your ambition, to be a new, ruling autocrat?"

"Not so much my ambition, but it's a role that history seems to have made for me, to serve the needs of a dangerous time on earth."

Josiah walked outside onto the portico and looked across the moonlit Bay. Thousands of house lights dotted the East Bay hills, the incandescent campfires of today's peasantry, huddled together, not fully understanding all the forces loosed in the world around them.

"Do you have to go on creating more slags?" he said. "Don't you have enough now?"

"Not nearly—I have less than two hundred actual slags among Foundation members right now, not including those pledged to Drost. They're all people in powerful government positions—and in first world to third world countries—but my slag recruiting process from among the ordinary members has been far too slow."

"Maybe Drost has been working day and night, also, slagging a larger battalion of his own followers."

"I don't think he'll be capable of doing that for some time. There was no beryllium left at Tupa Inca to manufacture the necessary strands."

"What if he threatens or buys off Hector to get at the beryllium we have in Larga?"

She smiled. "Hector has been slagged into my movement and he's already transferring the beryllium from Larga to another secret location where it's being stored under heavy guard."

Josiah sat in a chair on the portico and shook his head. There went his pension plan. "Will you try to manufacture more slagging materials?" he said. "You might be able to slag the entire world."

She put an arm around his waist. "No, Josiah; the complete technology for Drost's process and software may be impossible for me or anyone else to replicate. He really is a genius. I think the five thousand capsules I have will give me all the slags I need, but I intend to make doubly certain that Drost doesn't create any more of his own. I've set in motion a plan to bomb the Skatha facilities at Tupa Inca. It would suit us both, I'm sure, if Drost were in the facilities at the time. However, we must be prepared to face him again if he's not. You look troubled; you're not going to desert me now, are you?" She sat on his legs and slipped an arm about his neck. He held her and kissed her.

"I don't think I've felt this strongly about anyone before," he said. "We've been brought together, somehow, thankfully, to be with each other and to help each other with a critical mission—to destroy Drost. I wish it could stop right there. You make me uneasy, though, when you talk of your grand notions of going on to raise a force of dedicated followers to stamp out the terrorists of the world. I think you want to do it out of a selfless dedication to justice, but will anything faze you along the way? You'd make slags of people just as readily as Drost to accomplish your goals."

Vasthi sat up straight and protested, "There's a big difference here. I don't create slags to sate a personal appetite for lust. I want to increase their ability and dedication to help me bring justice to the world."

He shook his head. "You're so incredible with your single-mindedness about your mission. I hope I can get you to stop and enjoy some peace and quiet along the way."

She kicked off her shoes and straddled him on the chair, settling back onto her heels and holding him at arms' length. With a sigh she rose onto her knees and pressed her mouth to his. They struggled to adjust themselves to each other on the precarious limits of the chair and fell into an easy rhythm of movement.

Later that night Josiah and Vasthi took the elevator down one floor to the Hall of Molecular Light, accessible only to slags or those about to be initiated. A young woman placed flower garlands over their shoulders as they exited the elevator and hugged each of them in turn. A canopy of thousands of flowers festooned the ceiling and bushels of petals lay strewn across the floor. Two hundred or more people stood about dressed in white robes talking and drinking wine.

"How do you tell which ones are already slagged?" Josiah

said.

Vasthi reached out and caught the hand of a raven-haired woman. She smiled at the woman and held the woman's hand out to Josiah. "I wanted to show you her ordination ring; it is engraved with a likeness of the great Inca ruler, Tupa Inca. The ring signifies one who has attained the Molecular Light Priesthood. Carla, I'd like you to meet Josiah." Carla was a pretty, ochre-complexioned woman in her twenties. She leaned and planted a warm, moist kiss on Josiah's lips.

"You've come to us in very select company, Josiah. Our high priestess must think well of you." She glanced down at Josiah's hand. "So he's not ordained yet; will you personally ordain him tonight, Vasthi?"

"Yes, I wouldn't want anyone else to do it, though you would have been my choice otherwise," Vasthi said.

Carla smiled and clasped his hand. "Nice to have been introduced to you, Josiah. I must meet with our liturgical committee now and set tonight's ceremonies in motion. I'll have to say goodbye for now."

"They don't know what the slagging capsule actually contains, of course," Vasthi said after Carla had left. "They believe it to be a mind expanding drug passed down from the ancient Incas and which will free one's mind to receive the sacrament of slagging. They are taught slagging is the activation of inherent wisdom in a purified individual and brings forth in them a true knowledge of the universe. I believe an emphasis on mysticism over technology will promote greater loyalty and devotion in my slags— something Drost fumbled for with his Macnessa creation," she said, and smiled.

Soon after, the postulants were asked to present themselves to the Temple Scribe, who conducted them to their places for ordination. Vasthi held Josiah's arm and whispered to him, "Join the others and when the time comes I will act out the slagging ritual with you."

The scribe, a young man, placed his hand on Josiah's shoulder. "Welcome brother. Carla tells me you're to be honored by our High Priestess tonight. Follow me and I'll lead you to your place for the ceremony."

Josiah frowned at Vasthi, hesitated, and went with the scribe.

The postulants sat on the highly polished floor around a painted logo of the Sun God. Outside them sat the wider circles of slags, some playing Andean pipes, others drumming, and the rest chanting a litany of mantras to Mother Earth:

Gaia be saved,

Gaia be honored,

Gaia our beloved.

The plaintive rising and falling melody of the pipes reminded Josiah of the night in the mountains when Kepo played for him and Eila. Was she really gone? He felt an overwhelming sense of loss and sadness.

A dancer leaped onto the sun logo before Josiah. He was a powerfully built man and wore a helmeted headdress adorned with a profusion of curling, wispy black feathers and a flowing, sequined cloak of rainbow colors. He began a dance of robot-like, mechanical gestures, awakening gradually to flowing, sweeping movements, and in time to the steadily rising tempo of the pipes and drums. He crouched low, cupped a hand to an ear and pointed overhead. The drums picked up their tempo and overrode the pipes. The lights darkened and the dancer sprang upright and pulled his cloak back to uncover a sunburst medallion hanging on his chest. Strobe lights played on the medallion as the drums quieted and the pipes took over. The dancer went rapidly around the circle again in spinning, leaping movements and came thudding down in a crouch before a young woman. He swayed from side to side transfixing her with his stare so that she seemed to sway with him. He sprang upright again, exploding around the circle in leaps and bounds and landed in a crouch before Josiah.

The dancer's face leered, beads of sweat trickled from the bridge of his nose and spread beneath his eyes. He jerked a gleaming, broad-bladed knife from his belt and held it point up before Josiah's face. Josiah flinched but returned the stare. The blade passed slowly back and forth and Josiah felt sweat beading over his face. The sounds of pipes and drums and chanting rose in crescendo, till the dancer leaped away, turning round and round the circle, the strobe lights freezing him in the air at instants of time until he finally vanished from view during a momentary darkness.

Muscle spasms twitched in Josiah's face and shoulders as he calmed his labored breathing and relaxed his body. For a few moments it was like he had faced Drost covered in another man's skin. He thought he might have a seizure but the aura quickly faded and passed.

A woman walked onto the sun logo carrying a gold tray with several golden chalices, a gem-studded ceramic vase and a bowlful of opalescent capsules. She set the tray on the floor and Josiah's heartbeat quickened—the slagging capsules. Carla and a young man dressed like her in flowing white robes passed through the rings of postulants and into the logo area. Carla introduced herself and the priest with her, Yuri. The serving woman filled a chalice from the vase and handed it to Carla.

Carla took one of the slagging capsules, crushed it over the chalice, and beckoned to a male postulant. He rose quickly and came to her, took the chalice, and drank. The serving woman took the empty chalice from him and Carla smiled and placed her hands on the man's shoulders. She brought her face close to his and they embraced. Her lips found his, his arms and hands on Carla's back jerked and trembled, and a soft blue glow from overhead spotlights enveloped the two. The glow ebbed and pulsed repeatedly, till the tremors in the man's body stilled. She lifted back her head, smiled and touched his face, then took his hand and pressed a ring onto his finger. A new slag had been born and the crowd chanted praises.

Josiah watched as Yuri searched the faces of the postulants for the next candidate, when Vasthi stepped into the circle. She beckoned to Josiah. He rose slowly to his feet and stood with his arms held rigid at his sides. Vasthi accepted a chalice from the serving woman, took up a capsule and brought it over the chalice. She closed her eyes and looked up as if in prayer, then approached Josiah in a slow, easy stride. He felt his adrenalin hammer an alarm in his brain. She stood before him with the chalice and Josiah felt the sweat break out on his forehead. He noticed a half-dozen powerfully built men wearing gold-woven vests over bare torsos standing across the way.

"You know I can't be slagged," he whispered, anger biting into his voice.

Vasthi smiled, her eyes glazed as if in a trance. She whispered back, "Perhaps the Skatha reacted superstitiously to your brain wave aberrations," she said. "They never really tried, did they?"

"And if you do and it's fatal to me?"

She leaned her forehead against his shoulder. "I'm so afraid that in the end I shall lose you. If only I could really slag you into a devotee without risk to you, I would." She stood back and held the chalice out to him.

"I want to see the capsule," he said.

She reached to take his hand and he felt an unbroken capsule pressed into his palm. "Drink. It's only wine," she whispered. He took a breath and drank from the chalice. She turned to Carla who was watching. "I will complete Josiah's ordination in my room, since he is very special to me."

"Of course," Carla said. "Peace be to you," and all in the circle took up the peace refrain as Vasthi and Josiah walked away.

CHAPTER 17—Stadium

The next morning Josiah awoke in the penthouse suite of the temple to find Vasthi going through a stack of morning newspapers. He was startled to hear another voice in the adjoining room and rose to see a man through the open doorway, speaking into a radio transmitter. He recognized Mika, one of the intelligence officers he met aboard the ship anchored off the Galapagos. Mika removed his headphones and nodded.

Vasthi called to Josiah, "It's about time you're up. I need your reaction to some new developments."

"This is like living in a barracks,' he said, glancing again at Mika.

Vasthi got up from her chair and came over. "Really, there's no need to get upset about his being here. There's been some disturbing news this morning and I'm trying to keep on top of things. I thought it would help if I moved Mika into our place for a few days to maintain communications with my intelligence network, and by the way, he's even more devoted to me than previously. He's now a slag himself."

Josiah looked to observe his reaction but Mika seemed unperturbed, leaning back in his chair at the radio, smoking.

Vasthi sat on the bed beside Josiah. "I expect the next move will be up to Drost. I'd planned to bomb Tupa Inca tomorrow at dawn but the two aircraft we'd planned to use are being detained. They were flown to a small airfield in

Colombia to refuel and strike from there. A narcotics group runs the field but it was the best arrangement we could make on short notice. Unfortunately, government troops overran the field while our planes were there. I may have some difficulty explaining things and I've been trying to contact the right people in the government. In the meantime, I've suffered another disaster."

Josiah got up, strapped on his prothesis, pulled on a robe, and poured himself a coffee from a thermos on the room service cart. "Another disaster?"

"Yes, I had previously requested a demolition team dispatched to Ecuador as a backup plan. Drost engaged with them at Tupa Inca last night. He tore two of the commandos to pieces, fire-tongued another to ashes, and the commanding officer was relieved of his skin and identification papers. Only the one man escaped by hiding. Drost has probably long been aware that we've altered his slagging program. Since he doesn't have any more beryllium for slagging materials, his next tactic may be to try and recover the capsules I've taken." Vasthi got up from the bed, ran her fingers through her hair. and paced the room. "As soon as we get the planes released we'll strike at Tupa Inca again, but we must be prepared if the attack fails and Drost comes here."

"Tore them to pieces," Josiah mumbled, and set down his cup. "Good Lord." He glanced toward Mika in the other room. "He could be here already; that might be him there, in Mika's skin, just waiting to find out where you've hidden the slagging capsules before tearing us two apart."

"That sort of problem worried me, too, and I made radio contact two days ago with a government research scientist in

152

our intelligence lab, who also happens to be one of my slags. I provided him with all the technical factors I knew about slags and the Skatha, and the detection method he came up with in our brainstorming and experimentation was an isotope scanner. Our internal beryllium materials have low-level, long-term isotope emissions and he assembled a scanner in the lab that worked to detect it. We expect it would respond even more strongly to Skatha sheaths but we'll have to see. A few prototype devices may arrive today.

"It would be reassuring to know we could detect him if he's here," Josiah said. "What do we do—wait and see if he survives your air raid?"

"No, I've set myself a timetable of six months to slag the rest of the five thousand followers I want. I'm going ahead with those plans whatever else may happen."

"At your present rate it may take you another couple of years."

"I've tried to be too selective in the past. I wanted candidates that already held positions of strategic importance, people who already had access to power and money. Not that I'm avaricious but some wealth is necessary to achieve political goals. I'm altering our criteria to individuals with at least some potential, and trust they can gain positions of greater power and wealth later. After all, what humans can compete with a slag in matters of knowledge and analytic strategies?"

"So you're going to charge ahead—what's next?"

"I'm having Hector sell the remaining beryllium to help finance our movement."

"Our movement?"

"Come now, Josiah, I know you have serious reservations about the slagging, and I bear an awful responsibility for it, but the future of the earth and its environment depend on our success."

"So what is the plan?"

"To mobilize members from all the temples Eila had started around the world. They seem to have done well in the short time they've been in existence and they include thousands of enthusiastic new Foundation members, all possibilities for slagging. Our Inca trappings seem to have been quite fascinating to people. Some of my key slags are already on their way back to our overseas units. The small number of slags that Eila herself created and installed will be removed from their leadership posts so they won't present any serious problems to us. By tomorrow morning, the media in dozens of international cities will carry messages calling on members to assemble in San Francisco for a week of mass rallies at a sports stadium. It will be billed as a demonstration of solidarity and protest against the multinational businesses and industrial cartels that have coerced our governments into shameful silence about the destruction of the environment. We will charter airlines to carry all our members who want to attend this convention. Local members will organize tent cities along the Bay, in Golden Gate Park and other such places, anywhere they can find space." Vasthi paused to catch her breath, her face flushed with excitement.

Josiah scowled. "People are sure going to take notice of this new Inca invasion," he said. "This is not just a pep rally, I take it—you're going to try to complete your slagging at this

154

event?"

"Exactly, and we'll try to maintain some modest level of selectivity in our candidates. Our organizers will interview people each morning outside the stadium. We've worked for weeks designing and narrowing questions for twenty key screening criteria, including things like country, professional degrees, age, religion, financial assets, membership in other organizations, and especially any written recommendation by a temple leader. Data will be input to computers during the interview and candidates will receive their seat assignment. Afterward, temple leaders and I will scan the data, and make the most strategic choices to complete our slagging needs. Stadium attendants will circulate through the stands during the rallies and notify successful candidates where to report. The slagging ceremonies will be conducted in small tents on the field."

Josiah gathered up his clothes and carried them to the bathroom. It was almost too late to turn back. "You don't need to do this," he said from behind the door. "Just help me destroy Drost and try letting the Foundation achieve its goals without any more slagging."

"I want to secure a world of justice and peace and it can only be done by an overwhelming force of dedicated slags; I'm completely sure of this. You may have your scruples about slagging but it's the only way."

Mika interrupted, "Vasthi, a message from our agent in Guayaquil. Superintendent Hector has been found dead. The police are having to rely on DNA for identification—it seems he's been incinerated."

"Hector," Vasthi said, and her face was drawn. Josiah

came out from the bathroom and stared at Mika.

Mika read from the notes he'd taken. "Radio news reports said he'd been involved in the Inca Foundation and might possibly have died in an act of self-immolation. His motive is thought by the police to have been some sort of protest of industrial crimes against the environment."

Vasthi paced the floor. "And the stores of beryllium?"

"The police don't seem to be aware yet of its existence. However, we're taking the precaution of transferring it to a new storage site."

Vasthi looked out the tall windows at the morning sun rising above the East Bay hills. "The idiots—linking self-immolation with the Inca Foundation was ridiculous. We are activists, not pacifists; we destroy our opponents, not sacrifice ourselves to them." She turned to Mika, "Place our security forces on alert for Drost. As soon as the scanning devices arrive, check all visitors to the temple and send agents around to check the tent camps."

"The scanners have already arrived, and we'll get on with the surveillance right away. Also, you've been directed to report to a cabinet meeting tomorrow in the capitol."

Vasthi leaned against the window frame. "It's time to act. Have my secretary submit my resignation to the government immediately. The Inca Foundation is my life mission now."

"I'll see to all of it right away," Mika said.

"Come with me," she said to Josiah. "I'd like to go out to the stadium so that I might better anticipate the security and organizational problems that may arise. You might be able to

156

advise me in some areas, and besides, it may be safer for us to stay together. You could be next in line after me for Drost's vengeance."

"I doubt I'm very high on his list of concerns, though he probably wouldn't mind getting rid of me on general principles."

"You perhaps underestimate his fear of your Galactic Druid identity. Speaking of which, have you had any more visits with Akla that you haven't told me about?"

"Not since I left Ecuador last month," he said. "I don't know whether to be concerned or relieved."

Vasthi studied him for a few seconds. "Even the increased power of comprehension I've been given deals mostly with what has been learned and revealed by earlier mortals on earth. It would be unwise of me to doubt your nature, and perhaps you shouldn't doubt it too much either."

"I'm hoping my-on-the-job training will be enough to carry me through," he said.

They left the temple and drove to the sports stadium. The morning commute traffic was heavy and Vasthi drove as if pursued by a banshee, changing lanes constantly and closing on vehicles ahead until it seemed a crash was inevitable.

"Slow down or you'll kill us both before Drost ever sees us again," Josiah said.

"Never fear death," she said. "Pray only that you're never stupidly dispatched by an idiot," and she careened over into an adjoining lane. Tires squealed and a horn blew. A red

Lexus pulled abreast of them and a large-headed man shook a fist at them. Vasthi accelerated to cut him off and tires squealed again as he braked. Josiah turned and looked behind. The Lexus had dropped back about thirty feet and was staying there.

Josiah sagged in his seat. He hoped that if Drost pursued them here, he might be wrecked in traffic—car and beryllium shell hammered together and sold for recycling—and he, Josiah, could return to Ecuador to settle quietly into the golden harvest years he'd promised himself.

Mercifully within the next half-hour they arrived safely at the stadium and walked inside onto centerfield. Vasthi turned and looked about her at the soaring tiers of empty seats. Her face was radiant.

"Imagine," she said, "these stands filled to overflowing by my followers, my future slags, in just a few days from now. No despot on earth could withstand our rise. Our people will overthrow them from within their own ranks. Ours will be a worldwide revolution, without cannons, bombs, or other weapons of decimation."

"Those despots aren't likely to yield without a fight," Josiah said.

Vasthi dismissed his remark with a wave of hand, "Those that don't will of course have to be annihilated." She lifted her arms above her head and turned to all sides of the stadium, smiling, as if already accepting a tumultuous applause from the spectators.

"Who's going to control the ambitions of your slags if something should happen to you?" Josiah asked.

The exalted expression fled from her face. She lowered her arms and turned to face him. "What do you mean?"

She must have considered it and he wanted to work out a situation that bothered him. "Look, the slags have at their disposal all the accumulated scientific, philosophical, and sociological data known to man—but they've been programmed to interpret and apply that knowledge in a power-seeking, ends-justifying-the-means sort of behavior. The only brake on their personal ego is their programmed loyalty to you."

Vasthi shielded her eyes with a hand over her forehead, "Yes, yes—go on with your doubts."

"Well, putting aside your readiness to strike down a few hundred thousand or so terrorists, tyrants, and other thugs, you do have a personal ethic of reaching some just and peaceful society. But what if you're killed somewhere along the way? I mean, you're just as vulnerable as anyone else."

"Of course. I shall not even require a silver stake to the heart to go quietly into the night."

"Right, and if you're gone, each slag becomes a power-seeking individual, and a genius at making the best decision at every turn in a quest to secure that power. You'll let loose five thousand candidates for absolute dictator of the world and armies will march to the tune of bugles, drums, cannons and bombs as never before." He paused a moment. "Can you risk anything like that?"

Vasthi kept silent for a few moments. When she did speak, her voice was harsh. "Yes, I've considered it, but nothing of great value can ever be gained without great risk.

I must complete my mission before my life is over," she said.

CHAPTER 18—The Park

The frenzied preparations for the coming convention and accompanying anxieties that hung in the air seemed finally to tire Vasthi as the eve of opening day grew late. She and Josiah took their daily walk through rows of closely packed tents in Golden Gate Park sheltering many of the Foundation's international arrivals. Gusts of wind from an offshore weather front sent shudders across the slack canvas surfaces. It grew darker and gas lanterns sputtered into light within the tents, casting animated shapes of occupants against tent walls like a Thai shadow play.

"Well as far as numbers of attendees go, your expectations have been more than met," Josiah said.

Vasthi nodded as they continued to walk. "The time was ripe," she said. "Can you feel the excitement in the air? The entire crustal layer of consciousness on our planet seems to be in upheaval and ferment. Drost gave us a remarkable insight into creation when he described the ancient existence of the Dineen. The mantle of consciousness and energy overlying our planet has built up over eons of time and grows daily in thickness and complexity." She shuddered as if throwing off a chill. "Can it be any wonder that sociological and intellectual aberrations are also on the rise in this thickening pool of possibilities? Nevertheless, there are truths and natural law that will guide us, and we cannot be fainthearted when it comes to cutting out malignant cancers that subvert the law and corrupt souls."

They reached a paved walk and continued in silence for a few minutes. Vasthi stopped beneath a huge, arching bay tree and laid a hand on Josiah's shoulder.

"You've never told me that you loved me," she said.

He was surprised by the appeal and intensity of emotion in her voice and face and searched for a right answer. "I didn't think it would have mattered to you. Anyhow, my experience has been that if you find yourself marveling over being in love, you're only inviting the end of the relationship."

"You're being evasive. Don't you think we could make a life together?"

"I don't know if I could take the sort of mission you've envisioned for yourself. I've been stunned at my conscription into the Galactic Druid fraternity, but I'm just as stunned by you and what you're planning. It's like you're another time voyager who's been charged with shaking whole civilizations by the throat until they spit out their corruptions. We're totally different spirits. With luck, and maybe your help, I might succeed in doing what I have to do. But you—the task you've set yourself—that's so far beyond me that I get exhausted worrying about you because I do care for you."

"Did you love Eila?"

Josiah rubbed his temple. "That's complicated, too. We were close in the way that two lovers might be but there was still such a vast chasm between us. Who could think about whether it was real love?"

Vasthi shook her head and they continued walking. The evening air grew colder and they drew their woolen ponchos more tightly about them. They were passing a dimly lit tent pitched amongst some shrubs when a woman called to them.

"High Priestess, in here, please; I would have a word with you."

They stopped and turned. The woman was dressed in the variegated wrappings of a gypsy. She stood outside holding the tent flap open and beckoning for them to enter.

"I have little time madam; what is it you wish?" Vasthi said.

"Oh, but your Highness," soothed the woman, "this lowly one has been honored with a message for you concerning one who is in this world and yet not of this world." A bright smile showed in her dark countenance. Vasthi was startled by what she heard.

"Who told you to give me such a message?" Vasthi said.

The smile disappeared from the gypsy's face. "Don't be angry with me, Highness. There is more, but if my message is bitter to you I shall swallow it and suffer the wrath of the speaker. Go in peace, Highness," she said, scraping and bowing as she backed into her tent.

"Hold, you wretch," Vasthi said. She turned to Josiah, "I don't like the looks of this. Do you have the heat-sink gun?" Josiah nodded. "Come then," she said. "We shall see whether Drost is involved. Perhaps the time is at hand."

Josiah motioned to Vasthi to wait outside and he entered the tent first. He stood a few moments to adjust his eyes to the flickering glow of light in the dim interior. It seemed large and empty, save for a table with a lantern. Gradually, the shapes of trunks, crates, and standing rolls of rugs emerged from shadows around the walls of the tent.

Vasthi lifted the flap. "Does everything look all right?"

"Seems to, come in and let's talk with her."

Vasthi stepped inside and the old woman toddled behind, massaging her hands and crooning to herself.

"What's all this stuff in here?" Josiah asked.

"Only some wares to sell, Your Honor. Interested in a rug or some rare metals?" she asked.

"What kind of rare metals?" Vasthi said, grabbing hold of the woman's shoulders and shaking her.

The gypsy pulled from her grasp and backed away to the table, seeming frightened. "Why, gold and silver, Highness. Why would you be angry with me for that?"

"Something is not right, here," Vasthi said, moving about the open room and coming back to the table. "You wished to tell us something more?"

"Oh, yes, now I recall there was more. Please have a seat, Highness, while this old one catches her wits. I can scarcely think what it was I wanted to tell you." She bobbed about the table arranging a couple of chairs for Vasthi and Josiah. Exchanging glances, they sat, and Josiah turned to keep an eye toward the tent entry. The gypsy became highly agitated, pulling at her gloved hands and looking about, settling on Josiah.

"Perhaps your Honor would like to go outside and walk while two women chatter on about things?"

"No—get on with it," Vasthi said, slamming her hand on

164

the tabletop.

"There's no need for anyone to leave now," a voice droned from somewhere in the darkness.

"Drost," Vasthi shouted and leaped up. Josiah's chair tumbled back as he lumbered to his feet too. Lights came on and dozens of identical figures stared at them from all sides of the tent. "They're all images of Hiram, one of our men sent to Tupa Inca," Vasthi shouted. "What's happening?"

"I think he's using the Griffen's hologram projector," Josiah said. "Only one of them is Drost wearing Hiram's skin." He drew the heat-sink gun from inside his poncho.

Vasthi shouted, "Watch out, he's got the other heat-sink gun."

Laughter echoed through the tent as all the figures raised their weapons. "So, Josiah, who will you use your weapon on, which one, which one?" all the figures taunted. Josiah sighted at one figure and then jerked the barrel toward another. "Take a chance, Druid, fire at one of us. If you're lucky it will be the real Drost. If not, my answering shot will deliver you the horror of existing for a very long time as a slab of rock. But as for you, Vasthi—you, I'll give a chance to repent. You've stolen my slagging capsules—return them to me and I'll forgive you. Perhaps I'll even find a way to calm that disturbing unrest in your spirit. Think about it, but you haven't much time. For now, I must mete out Josiah's punishment. Watch and repent, my testy child."

The voices fell out of synchronization and clashed and reverberated. Josiah gritted his teeth and tried to pick a target. The figures mocked him, eyes wide, voices chortling with laughter as they plodded forward and raised their weapons.

"There, Josiah—there," Vasthi shouted, pointing her slag scanner at one of the figures. "That one, shoot—shoot!"

Josiah aimed in the direction she pointed. The figures surrounding him all activated and rays crisscrossed the room as Josiah dove to the floor while firing at his chosen target. A kerosene lamp arced toward the same target and exploded over it. The ring of figures staggered ahead unable to see through the smoke and burning fabrics. Josiah fired again at the target he'd locked onto. All the figures of Drost screamed and clutched their shoulders, falling backward into a blanket of flames racing about the tent. Josiah got up and tried for another shot but flames leaped out from the walls of the tent, fanned by draughts of wind rushing through the entry. The outer stay ropes parted and the burning tent shook and flapped wildly in the wind.

"Let's go, we've got to get out of here," Josiah shouted to Vasthi.

"No, wait, we've got to finish him, we've got to be sure," she said.

"It's no use." He pulled her toward the entrance, choking in the smoke and unsteady on his prosthesis as he tried to hold her.

The tent collapsed in a flaming mass minutes after they'd staggered outside, coughing and bleary-eyed. They circled warily around the tent with the heat gun concealed beneath Josiah's poncho, as figures gathered from all sides to watch the blaze.

166

"Damn these people," Vasthi said. "They've given cover to Drost if he escaped the flames."

"Nothing to be done about it," Josiah said. "Let's just hope he didn't get out."

They continued around the tent, threading their way through the encirclement of onlookers, scanning faces in the flickering light of the fire, coughing in smoke as the wind shifted. The fire department arrived and hosed down the flames. Josiah and Vasthi watched as the firemen worked their way through the charred, smoldering contents—half-burned rugs, two storage trunks, blackened electronic gear—pitching articles to the side as they searched for any survivors. A helmeted fireman came out from the debris and reported to a Fire Chief.

"There doesn't seem to have been anyone inside," he said.

"Well, that's fortunate," the Chief said. "I warned the Mayor we'd be in for something like this if we didn't stop this ragtag occupation of the park. This cult must be pulling strings with someone to get permission for allowing such outrageous conditions."

Josiah and Vasthi didn't wait to hear any more. They left and walked toward a thoroughfare to get a taxi.

"He got away somehow," Vasthi said. "I wonder how badly you might have injured him?"

"Hard to say—I didn't paint him for more than a few seconds before the flames swallowed him up."

"He'll try again if he's able to, of course," Vasthi said. "He

167

has to act quickly before I succeed in slagging more followers into my service."

"You're probably right." Josiah became lost in thought and lagged behind as they walked.

Vasthi turned and glanced back. "What's the matter?"

"The gypsy woman—it must have been her! She must have thrown the lamp at the real Drost just as he was going to freeze me into oblivion."

"I hadn't given it a thought until you mentioned it," Vasthi said. "I've been so vexed at Drost's escape when it looked like we had him. But you're right, she's got to be the one who saved us."

"Do you suppose she could have been—"

"Eila? I wonder. I thought I'd finished her with that blast from my heat-sink gun, but the Skatha may be more impervious to a blast than our ex-friend, the Macnessa. I searched for a sign of her in the water after she fell from the Griffin, but I never spotted anything."

Josiah was pained thinking about the event.

"Anyhow, if it was her," Vasthi said, "Drost isn't likely to forgive her this new lapse of loyalty. Her attachment to you may have made her totally untrustworthy for his purposes now."

"If Eila is still alive I'd like to see that she gets the beryllium Hector produced from the ore," Josiah said.

"To take it back to Aquama—why not? But be cautious

about being lured onto that spaceship when she's ready to go. She might decide to take along an extra passenger." Vasthi's voice was sharp and irritable and she turned away to hail a taxi.

CHAPTER 19—Apostates

After the first day of the convention Vasthi and Josiah returned to the upper rooms of the temple. The planned number of people for that day had been successfully slagged without any hitches and Vasthi was pleased. They sat with their drinks in gold fabric cushioned, carved wood chairs.

"Everything is going so well," she said. "I can hardly believe our success. But where is Drost—what's happened to him? What is he up to?"

"It puzzles me, too," Josiah said. "He's let you slag a lot of new followers today without incident. Something is wrong. Maybe he'll let this go on all week and then bring down some disaster on everyone in the stadium. But why not immediately, so that he could grab the rest of your slagging material to convert back to his own use?"

"He'd have a difficult time locating all the capsules—they've been dispersed. A courier brings me a part of the supply each day and the rest stays hidden at different locations."

"When and where's the next pickup?"

"Tomorrow, but it's better that you don't know any more than that. He might be a cruel interrogator if he had you and sensed that you knew."

"What about you?"

"That's unavoidable, isn't it? He'll always be a threat to me until I put him away."

"We have the same mission of destroying him so we might as well share the risks. I want to make the next pickup."

"Very well," she said after a long pause. "I'll explain our security arrangements. They're a little elaborate, but I credit them with having frustrated any efforts by Drost to recover the capsules so far. It's likely that things can't continue that way, and I suspect we'll encounter him before another day or two passes." She got up from her chair, walked to a small, carved walnut desk, and flipped through an appointments book. "Last week's pickup came from an airline bus terminal locker in downtown. Tomorrow's will come from a historic Chinese workers' temple in the river delta area east of the city."

"Quite a shift. If he's got people watching your movements that might throw them off."

"We'll see; with Drost I don't think it's ever a good idea to underestimate his cunning. Are you sure you want to do this? You might get your wish to encounter him."

Josiah was silent. He ran his fingers through his hair, got up, and walked over to the window to look out over the Bay. "Like I said, we need to share the. What time, and how do I find this place?"

"You should leave about four A.M. tomorrow morning. Mika will drive for you and you'll be followed by a car of Special Forces men, formerly with our military."

"Slags now, I suppose?"

172

"Yes, but you'll have the chance to face Drost yourself if he should try to intercept the pickup. I'll instruct Mika and the others. If you need help they're ready to defend you with their lives."

"Okay, let's go over the setup."

Vasthi took a map from the drawer. She spread it out on the desktop and Josiah looked on as she traced the route from the city.

"Here, in Louke. It's almost a ghost town now. Built a long time ago by Chinese laborers coming off the finished railroad construction or from the gold fields to labor on farms in the region. At one time there were gambling, opium, and girls there, but you won't see anything like that now. Only a few blocks of old buildings and a handful of elderly Chinese. One of the old buildings is a historic temple which houses a number of religious trappings and relics sent over from China. It also served as a sort of justice court, where the town elders sat in judgment on grievances between Chinese. A cache of slagging capsules is hidden in the judgment room. The caretaker will lead you to it after you give the password I arranged with him."

"You sure picked an obscure out of the way place."

"We know that some of Drost's slags are here in the city watching us so we have to be very careful. Anyhow, the caretaker will at some time say to you, 'freewill is truly a penance,' and you will reply, 'slagging is our absolution.'"

"Very pointed exchange," Josiah said.

Vasthi opened another drawer in the desk and handed him an isotope scanner. "Take no chances. You should scan not only your own escort party, but also the caretaker and anyone else you make contact with on this trip. Drost might not have the sheath of the army officer he wore in the tent." She paused a moment and touched his face. "And remember, too, if Eila is really alive don't be too quick to trust her. Maybe it really was her who saved our lives in that tent, but she's shown herself a confused woman with divided loyalties. Remember, it was she who lured us into that tent."

Josiah's expression grew pensive. "We had such a deep friendship from the very beginning, but you're right. She is torn between divided loyalties. I'll just have to be careful."

Later that evening they went together to a discussion group held amongst the newly ordained priests. Only twenty were to be there, all by special invitation.

"What's the significance in those you invited?" Josiah asked as they descended in the elevator.

"As it was with Drost, it seems I'm to be faced by a few apostates in the ranks of my slags. It was not entirely unexpected. As Drost found with me, a small part of our population has exhibited a free will that apparently can't be programmed out of existence with our slagging cocktail.

"Is there anything you've found unique about them?" he said.

The elevator stopped and the door opened. Vasthi paused, staring out at the temple room. "Yes, there is. I'd formed some tentative opinions over the past few weeks after questioning some of our earlier slags. I've also examined the questionnaires of today's slags and spoke briefly with the respondents to evaluate some of my earlier

174

opinions."

Josiah took her arm and stepped from the elevator with her. "And?"

"It was rather paradoxical," she said as they walked across the floor toward the group of slags seated on cushions surrounding the sun logo. "One striking observation was that the troublesome slags were all ultraconservative practitioners of established, dogmatic religions—Catholics, Jews, Muslims. "Would you have expected that?"

"I would have guessed it would be the freethinkers who would resist giving their unquestioned allegiance," Josiah said.

She stopped short of the circle and faced him. "Exactly but think about it. Freethinkers and humanists have noted all the chaos and betrayals of the established religions. Their response has been to give themselves completely over to the scientific and humanistic idealism of our movement, even when it demands subservience to a charismatic leader."

"Perhaps it doesn't say much for their powers of critical thinking."

"No more than it does for the religious fundamentalists. The fundamentalists defy anything in history that could challenge their revealed beliefs. Millions of pious Jews consumed in the Holocaust, flood and famine routinely decimate millions of devout Muslims in Bangladesh and Africa, and a few percent of Catholic oligarchs own South America while millions of their brethren live and die in poverty. it requires a strong exercise of freewill to continue belief despite the evidence of such disasters."

"Are you a religious fundamentalist?"

"I was—when I was a child. I soon became a skeptic about following any of the traditional religions." She took his arm and continued on, leaving him in the outer circle of slags while she passed through their ranks to the center of the sun logo. All bowed and took seats on the floor.

Vasthi remained standing to address them. "Why do you suppose I've summoned you particular priests to meet with me here this evening?"

Murmurs went around, a few nervous shrugs and coughs, and a dark-skinned young Asian got to his feet.

"I wondered that very thing, High Priest."

"You may call me Vasthi."

"Thank you, Vasthi. I had looked around and talked with these others before you arrived and I made some few observations. May I speak of them?" he said.

"Go on, Ashok," she said, and sat on the floor.

Ashok smiled easily and gestured about toward his comrades, "We all seem to be of a ritualistic nature, the obvious expression of which is our professed religions. But to my mind, those choices were most often accidental, or circumstantial." He paused to smile as numerous listeners whispered protests, and he dismissed them with a wave of his hand. "Believe as you will, brothers and sisters, but there is perhaps more underlying the nature of many in this room than the happenstance of being counted in church, temple, or mosque. Quite apart from the conventional liturgies that soothe our fellows and only mildly sustained us, there may

176

be deeper rituals among us—"

A thin, spindly man interrupted him. "There are indeed deeper rituals that live within us, or should," he said. He bounded to his feet and peered from deep-set eyes beneath thick brows. "We are all servants of the one, universal God and Him only should we call Master." His voice grew tremulous. "Wondrous stores of knowledge have been bestowed on us with our initiation into the Incan priesthood, but there seems a permeation of evil may also have corrupted our senses. Why should we feel compelled to recognize Vasthi as our supreme authority—even before our submission to the omniscience of the Holy One? What spell have we fallen under? When her voice commands, I feel almost powerless to question. Once before, the Evil One in the guise of a serpent tempted a woman to bring about mankind's fall." He paused and turned from Ashok to Vasthi. "It must not happen again," he said, and drew a pistol from a shoulder bag.

He was too far for Josiah to reach him when the man aimed at Vasthi. In a blur, Ashok was behind him and threw a running silk noose tightly around the man's throat. He dropped the pistol and clawed at the noose, his voice choking and rattling till he grew silent and slumped back against Ashok.

A shocked, ashen-faced Vasthi rose to her feet. "A curious expertise for a man of religion," she said to Ashok.

"But an altogether holy act, Vasthi," he said, coiling the noose. "You have heard of our devotees in northern India called Thuggee, those who worshipped Kali, Goddess of Destruction and Rebirth?"

Vasthi threw off a shiver. "Let us hope this unfortunate incident can be adequately represented to the authorities."

"Are the Thuggee ritual killings so different from the ritual killings of war sanctioned by other religions and nationalisms? I think not, Vasthi, but I shall be your loyal devotee at whatever you sanctify. If not Kali, you are surely the same side of the one godhead from which she sprang and I say this only in love."

Vasthi frowned at Ashok's repeated references to Kali but the depth of his loyalty andevotion awed her.

CHAPTER 20—Louke

The telephone woke Josiah at precisely four A.M. He bolted upright in bed and looked about. As soon as he had a sense of time and place he lifted the receiver.

Mika said, "We have the car waiting at the temple entrance, Sir."

"I'll be ready in ten minutes," Josiah said and hung up. He sat on the edge of the bed and strapped on his prothesis.

Vasthi stirred. "Is it time already?" Drowsiness slurred her speech.

"Yes, but there's no need for you to get up yet. I'll see you at the stadium when I return from Louke." She'd already fallen back to sleep.

Josiah left the temple and walked to the two waiting cars. Ashok got out of the front seat of one and opened the rear door for him. He paused a moment to look at Ashok's smiling, amiable face and shuddered when getting into the car. As quick as he was settled, the car shot forward and swerved onto the street running parallel to the waterfront. Josiah caught a glimpse of the car carrying the Special Forces men turn the corner behind them. He felt in his pocket and took out the isotope scanner. Guardedly, he aimed it at the back of Ashok's head, then Mika's. Two slag readings, he slid the device back into his pocket and let out a breath.

Ashok turned around. "I asked High Priestess if I might go

with you this morning to help guard your safety. I heard her tell Mika last night in the parking lot that he was to drive you on a mission that might endanger your life." He kept watching Josiah as if hoping for an explanation of what the mission or danger might be. Josiah only nodded and Ashok turned around again.

They drove on in silence. The journey took them over the Bay Bridge and down long, lightly trafficked stretches of freeway. The narrow belt of low coastal mountains quickly gave way to rolling, grassy hillsides, long stretches of flatland, and an hour later, crossing another bridge, past the low-lying river delta of islands and marshlands. The sky was already lit with dawn when they reached Louke. The weathered wood buildings stood like blackened ships anchored against a copper burnished sky. A rough, timbered boardwalk fronted the buildings for several blocks along the main street. Mika watched the addresses as they drove by and stopped the car in front of a building with a small garden area of ancient, twisted oaks at one side.

"Sir, this is the place," Mika said.

Josiah studied the building before getting out. He waited with Ashok while Mika collected the two men from the other car, then walked behind them and surreptitiously checked everyone with his scanner. On reaching the building and finding no entrance from the boardwalk, they went along a stone pathway through the garden. The ground between the trees was overgrown with coarse grasses and the stone walk showed no disturbance on its red, lichen-blotched surface. They arrived at an ivory-knobbed wood door and Josiah knocked. They waited, with no sounds but the soughing of wind through leafless trees. Josiah was about to knock again when the door opened. His hand gripped the scanner in his pocket but he shook off his tension when he reasoned that the skin of this slight, gnarled, wizened old man in front of him couldn't possibly accommodate Drost's stature.

"Vasthi said you'd be expecting us," Josiah said.

The old man bowed slightly and opened the door wider. "It's very early. but welcome."

The security men remained outside and Josiah, Mika, and Ashok entered the building. They waited a moment till the old man closed the door and led them down a short hallway to the entrance of a large room. He stood aside as Josiah and the others entered the dimly lit room. A light came from votive candles arrayed before an alcove of dolls dressed in silk-brocaded robes at one end of the room. A sweet scent of incense permeated the still air. Josiah walked over to observe two life-sized dolls, one heavily jeweled, an emperor perhaps, the other a gaudily painted mythological god or demon. He was startled when the old man coughed at his side. Josiah waited expectantly for the first line of the code but the old man only fidgeted about, hands clasped behind his back.

"Is there anything you have heard of in our temple that you might wish me to show you," the old man said.

Josiah's suspicion rose and his nerves felt jangled. "I understand that there's a sort of courtroom that the early settlers used?" he said.

"Yes, yes—the Room of Judgments. Please follow me and I will show you." He padded off toward a doorway in the far corner of the room.

Josiah hesitated, something was wrong or he'd have been

given the code by now. He signaled to the others, "Mika, come with me. Ashok, you remain here and if we don't return or get word back to you in ten minutes, get the security people and come looking for us. Something isn't right." The old man was already through the door and Josiah hurried after him.

They walked down a corridor to another doorway. As Josiah followed the old man through the opened door, the point of a blade pressed into his side and a hand gripped his shoulder. "Please don't make any sudden moves that may cause me to disembowel you," a man said in a courteous voice. Another man held Mika at gunpoint and relieved him of his pistol. Josiah's captor frisked him and removed the heat-sink gun and scanner. Josiah panicked at the thought of encountering Drost without his weapon.

A dull morning light beamed into the room from narrow, horizontal windows near the ceiling. Josiah darted a few glances about as he was prodded ahead—no other doorway but the one they'd entered. A continuous row of high-backed, dark mahogany chairs stood out from each wall along the length of the room.

A voice spoke out, "Leave Josiah with me and take the other outside with you."

The two men prodded Josiah toward a slumped figure seated in one of the chairs near the center of the room and left him. Josiah strained to recognize the figure in the dust-speckled light as he drew near. His chest tightened—it was the face of Hiram, the identity Drost wore in the tent.

"We meet again, Druid," Drost said in a low, rumbling voice.

182

He stared at Josiah for several minutes, not speaking, and Josiah felt the perspiration trickle from his brow and armpits.

"Vasthi is my real enemy," Drost said. "I need have no quarrel with you. I would remind you that there have been times past when Galactic Druids have found accommodation with powerful rulers of the Universe."

And paid dearly for their cowardice, came the voice of Akla from somewhere deep in Josiah's brain. That price was the end of their eternal cycle.

"You have only to reveal where Vasthi has hidden my property and you will be richly rewarded," Drost said.

"How did you find out about this place?" Josiah said, bidding for time and hoping for Ashok's arrival with the security men.

"From one of my slags, a classmate of Vasthi at the Galapagos conference. He lives in this region now and has been reporting to me on the activities of the San Francisco temple since its inception. He reported several visits by Vasthi to this place and I instructed him to find out whether she might be hiding the slagging capsules here. However, no sign of them was found here. He had her followed further and observed her visits to an airline terminal as well. It then became suspect that she may have dispersed the slagging capsules at several locations."

"Is the old man the caretaker of this place?" Josiah asked.

"No, I tried to force the real owner of the temple to tell us where the materials were, but it's been unsuccessful. The owner is a retired tong boss from the City and Vasthi had him slagged into her service. The old man is only his servant

183

and we had him greet you—" he paused, "while his employer recovers from his unfortunate show of resistance. I suppose Vasthi gave you some sort of passwords you were to exchange?"

Josiah kept glancing toward the doorway. What was keeping the security men? "If the owner couldn't tell you anything, why would you think I know any more than him?"

Drost leaned an elbow on the chair arm and propped his chin. "You'll confide in me because you'd rather not undergo any more unspeakable trials to resist." He said and smiled. "You'll cooperate, and after we take possession of the stolen slagging capsules we'll see whether Vasthi herself might attempt a pickup. I can be patient in awaiting a final encounter with her. What is your decision, Druid? You can also help me to recover the processed beryllium that Hector has hidden somewhere in Ecuador. Will you join with me?" His eyes narrowed and he leaned forward in his chair. "Speak—or I may soon relieve you of that faculty. Do you have hopes the men you left outside will rescue you? I destroyed them moments after you entered the temple." Drost reached beside the chair and raised his heat-sink gun.

Josiah jerked backward when a blur of a figure rose from behind Drost's chair and a running nose whistled in the air to encircle Drost's throat.

"It's no good, Ashok—get away quickly," Josiah shouted. Drost cried out as the noose sliced into the neck of his human sheath and the pain registered to his inner being. He lurched to his feet in a wild rage, dragging Ashok over the back of the chair. In the throes of searing pain, Drost dropped the heat-sink gun and stabbed his fingers under noose and skin. He ripped the noose free as he tore off half his face. He staggered to the fallen Ashok, crouching wide-eyed, bewildered and paralyzed with fear. Drost dragged Ashok to his feet as Josiah recovered the heat-sink gun from the floor."

"Let him go or I'll shoot," Josiah shouted.

Drost turned fear-glazed eyes on him as Josiah armed the heat-sink gun and took aim. With an enraged scream, Drost lifted Ashok and hurled him onto Josiah, sending both crashing to the floor. Drost prepared to attack when Mika staggered into the room, disheveled and disoriented, holding the other gun. Drost turned and splintered through the outside wall as Josiah fired another beam at him.

"After him," Josiah shouted, and followed through the broken wall. Mika and Ashok came close behind and they ran through the garden and onto the street. Rain drizzled from a now heavy, gray sky and banks of tule fog rolled in from the river. Josiah turned in circles, gun outstretched, water beading on his face. "Can you see him?"

"No," Ashok said, his voice rasping, still frightened by the sight of Drost's torn face and the great strength of his frenzy. "Let us get the materials Vasthi sent you for, Sir, and leave quickly. The beast is gone but what was it, really?"

"It's a long story. Let's go back in and find the real caretaker. The old man we met was a servant." Josiah took one more look up and down the street. He shook his head, murmuring in his breath, and the two men went back into the temple.

CHAPTER 21—Crustal Life

When Drost came to his senses four days later, he was waist-deep in river water, slumped against a mud bank and surrounded by canebrake. He straightened, felt the distress in his inner being, and splashed higher onto the bank.

"The heat-sink gun has done some damage," he whispered into the murky dusk descending over the river. He tried moving his limbs, one by one. He had complete use, but the pain from his torn human sheath triggered waves of nausea. He lifted his hand to gaze at the skin, purplish and bloated, and tucked in his chin straining to see where he'd torn away his hood of flesh, the edges now bleached and pulpy. He removed and set aside his clothing and laid back into the soft mud bank, burrowing, until it almost closed over him. The numbing shock of the heat-sink ray had waned and the pain of the torn sheath intensified. He sat up and with retching gasps and cries of pain clawed at the remaining neck of the sheath with both hands. He brought his electro-biotic charge to maximum intensity and the skin burned between his hands as he passed them down his body. Twice, the shock transmitted from the ravaged sheath to his brain almost caused him to lose consciousness. In a few minutes he'd torn and burned the remainder of the sheath away and lay back again, gasping in the mud. Gradually, the residue of pain, disgust, confusion and doubt subsided.

The human bitch had won that chapter. She'd defeated a Lord of the Universe though she was less than a light-year removed from the consciousness of a rock.

He let out a scream and a flock of mud hens burst from the canebrake and rose frantically into the air, squawking at the grotesque invader splayed out on their riverbank. He watched dimly as they disappeared in the dull gray sky and lifted an arm to bring the flesh-encrusted watch to his face.

Four days. Four days lying here with this putrid human sheath rotting on him. He struggled upright, lifting himself free of the sucking mud ooze, went to the edge of the flowing water and cleansed his body. He dressed again in his ripped clothes, checked his GPS coordinates on the command module, and stumbled along the bank headed north.

In twenty minutes, he reached an area of flattened canebrake and checked his position again. After looking in all directions he called down the Griffin. A great sense of relief flooded over him as the craft descended, becoming almost an indiscernible object in the vapory mists. It settled onto the canebrake and the LED-powered pigmentation activated over its smooth surface, mimicking the shifting colorings and shapes of the canebrake. He staggered forward through the flattened growth surrounding the Griffin and leaned against it.

He needed to leave this planet. The pleasures derived were not worth the danger to his existence. There would be other more amenable outposts in the Universe where the inhabitants would welcome him and perhaps be more pliant subjects for his needs. His breath came in short gasps and he slid into a seated position, cradling his head in an arm held against the craft. His thoughts came and went as in a fever.

First, he would repay them for their treachery. By now, Vasthi had completed building her Foundation and he would

188

have to raise a more powerful force against her. Think—think of how this might be done. There was only one force on this planet that would be greater than the army of slags he'd lost to her, and it slept until its time should come again. He would cheat the evolutionary clock that eventually molded all spent creatures into inert rock, waiting to be summoned to a future life again.

"Yes, yes—I am Drost, I exist, I can subdue time and evolution," he cried, sitting up and raising his fists to the sky. "I can do it; I can raise the Dineen once again to do my bidding and defeat my enemies."

He staggered to his feet and his breath came in shallow gasps as he held out the command module. Pointing it at the craft, he activated it repeatedly, drunkenly, long after the hatch door had already hissed open. He laughed, grasped the sides of the hatchway and hauled himself into the Griffin, dripping and muddy. The hatch hissed shut, blue reaction lights came on, the engine throbbed into life, and the Griffin lifted into the sky.

Drost was incautious in his mad haste back to Tupa Inca and several airline pilots reported sightings of a glowing blue orb searing across the night sky. He monitored the last pilot's radioed report. What did it matter now? If Josiah were to reveal all he knew of the Skatha, perhaps no more than a handful of eccentric people would believe him. In any case he'd soon be leaving this insidious planet after setting in motion the accelerated downfall and enslavement of the human race by the infinitely superior Dineen.

As soon as he landed at Tupa Inca and secured the Griffin below ground, he hurried down the corridors, past the lab and metal plant, and on to his quarters. Eila waited for him. She appeared startled to see him in tattered clothing and without his sheath.

"What has happened?" she said in alarm.

"The meddlesome Druid thwarted my plans," he said, dropping onto a chair and shielding his eyes. "He was fortunate to have caught me with a ray from a heat-sink gun. I've lain stunned for four days on a riverbank."

"Have you killed him?" she said, her eyes wide.

"No," he said, his voice a growl, vexed at having to admit such a failure. "But how did your mission go—have you located where Hector shifted the beryllium?"

She let out a breath. "Yes, it was being held in an closed-down warehouse. I've bribed their security and our workers have been transporting the beryllium here for the past several days. We'd have plenty of fuel for the Epoch-3 to reach Aquama, and a trove of extra metal to hand over to our leaders. I'm glad you've agreed to leave. If we stayed things could end terribly—for everyone."

"Nevertheless, we'll stay long enough to hasten the ultimate subjection of the perfidious, base people of this planet. I am going to set in motion the immediate awakening of the Dineen," Drost said.

"You can do that?" Eila said, shocked. "But think of all the research and experiments you did to raise and create just that one vile distortion of a Dineen, the Macnessa."

"I learned much during that research and I've found that scientists of the United States are engaged in a project that will assist my goal. It will provide me with the means to free hordes of Dineen from their cosmic imprisonment."

Eila sat and buried her face in folded arms on a table. "What is happening in Josiah's country and what must we do before we can leave here?"

"The American scientists plan to store radioactive wastes from nuclear power plants, deep into rock formations. It's exactly the sort of energy we need to hasten the rise of Dineen consciousness to a necessary level for animate existence. The energy released by decay elements of the radioactive waste can provide an infinitely greater energy source than the Dineen receive from the natural radioactivity of the Earth's crust. We will refocus that waste energy to our purpose."

"Are the Dineen everywhere?" Eila said, lifting her head. "Perhaps this waste storage project is far removed from their presence."

Drost reached for a small tin of narcotic-laced beryllium supplement lying on the table. He took a pinch and tucked it behind his lip structure. "An inanimate consciousness lies over the entire face of this planet," he said. "Their own philosophers, Jung and others, have tried to explain this. No matter where one might look, seeds of ancient, animate life are waiting to rise again from the molecular pool impregnated within the crustal surface. The Dineen are closest to an animate state, and the place chosen for the earth's first nuclear waste repository is in a rock formation particularly rich in their presence. The repository is now completely filled with nuclear waste and in three months workers will begin sealing access to it. I must act before then."

"How would they emerge from their imprisonment without your intervention?"

"The Earth gives birth to its creatures as it always has. Throughout the millennia of creation it has heralded such events with great earthquakes, grinding and tearing at its fabric in its throes of pregnancy, giving birth to the ancient reptiles and dinosaurs, and to humans in turn, all spewed from the crust of its belly. Even today earth's scientists fail to see the significance of large areas of Earth's crustal uplifting, and the growing number of major earthquakes along pregnant fault lines spanning its surface. The labor pains of the natural regeneration of the Dineen have already begun to stir within this planet, but I will hasten it."

She was spellbound. "When would they otherwise be reborn?"

"In the natural course of evolution, perhaps not for a few hundred millennium, and so my thirst for revenge cannot wait on evolution. You remember the isotope accelerator and amino gas synthesizer I used to create the Macnessa? It has become apparent to me how they might be modified to combine with the enormous amount of radioactive waste energy concentrated in the repository. I may succeed in awakening an army of the Dineen in anywhere from several weeks to several months, but we need to act quickly because the repository is full with waste and ready to be sealed."

Eila rose and paced the room. "What if the repository is sealed before you can accomplish your goal?"

"There is that possibility, of course. Still, although the Dineen will ultimately settle the fate of all on this planet, I want to witness the destruction of Vasthi and the Galactic Druid before we leave." He sighed and closed his eyes, feeling the drug's hit on his brain. "I have a great deal to do now," he said, "I hope to have our equipment ready in one week, but I'll need your help. Have the rest of the bio-metallic research apparatus brought from the Epoch-3 to my laboratory. Dismantle the backup ionic gas generator from the spaceship's armory. I'll need that and one of the spare beryllium power modules from the ship." Without waiting for Eila's response, he walked from the apartment to the laboratory.

Drost worked furiously over the next few days. It was usual for him to ingest a few grams of beryllium supplement each day to make up for normal Skatha body metabolism, but now he found it necessary to triple his intake—and often laced with narcotic enrichments. He felt the strain on his inner organic being, particularly on his mind. He was hallucinating much more frequently now and at times found himself wandering off on experiments completely anomalous to his immediate objectives. At one point he awakened from a trance to find himself experimenting with the creation of coexisting liquid life systems. Two dissimilar liquids, each with apparent creative thought processes, when placed in a common solution established territorial boundaries, made war, commingled, exhibited miscegenation—he looked up from the sub-electron scanning microscope and shook his head. "Fascinating," he murmured drunkenly, and swept the glass vials and apparatus crashing to the floor. He went back to work on the amino gas synthesizer that would give life to the Dineen.

At the end of the week he'd finished a prototype. It was fairly large, several cubic feet in volume, and would best be miniaturized further for transport. But first, its performance should be tested. The energy source was the beryllium oxidation reactor and he inserted a measure of beryllium pellets in the reactor's fuel chamber. As he connected the output nozzle of the synthesizer to a spectroscope, Eila entered the laboratory.

"How much longer?" she said, wandering about and inspecting the experimental setup.

I'm testing the first component now," he said, as he programmed a miniscule flow from the synthesizer. "This step requires a great deal of caution. The fuel reaction in the synthesizer develops an enormous flow vortex. At full flow conditions it could suck in every cubic foot of air in this laboratory and convert it to an amino acid complex, the building block of life."

He looked up from his work and watched her. Eila seemed listless and distracted. "What's troubling you?" he said.

"Nothing," she said, barely whispering. She swept her long tresses of silver hair back over her shoulders and he caught his breath.

"When was the last time we made love?" he said.

"Have we ever? I prefer not to remember."

"You're so disinterested. You've never even worn a human sheath. Don't you ever yearn for the heightened sensual pleasure it could bring?"

Eila's expression became more irritated and she resumed pacing about the lab, almost upsetting a cart full of vials and test tubes. "I have no need of wearing a human sheath," she said in a harsh voice.

"Is that so?" he said. His eye apertures narrowed and accentuated an intensity of light within. He had not taken another sheath since his painful shedding of the one worn at Louke. In contrast to Eila's delicate, many hued jewel-like countenance, his facial features shone as a dull yellowed gray variation of the beryl silicate plating. The multi-faceted planes of his forehead and cheeks were broader than Eila's, and bore a much duller sheen, but his visage seemed sculpted to classic Roman proportions.

"I may have neglected your female desires for too long a time," he said. "Perhaps you'd enjoy coupling now?"

"Don't be a fool," she said. "What pleasure could you derive from that—you wear no sheath."

"Do you imagine that I've enjoyed my sheathed sex with humans for so long that I've forgotten my duty toward you? No matter that I'll take diminished sensual pleasure in it. Your own, inner stimulus receptors remain quite responsive to coupling. So, tell me what's wrong? During the long, dark days of our voyage here you seemed more willing to have me join with you. Perhaps you have been serviced more adequately by the Galactic Druid?" He reached out and grabbed her arm.

"You're loathsome," she said, stiffening her stance against his grip, her eyes wide. "Let me go."

"What was it like with him," he said.

"I have nothing to tell you."

He yanked at her arm. "I don't know if I can trust you with

195

anything. I still find it hard to believe it was Vasthi who threw the lamp in that tent," he said.

She pulled free from his grip. "The Aquama elders sealed us as paramates for the duration of our space expedition," she said. "But you've made a mockery of those pledges since we arrived on this planet. The bond enjoined on us by our leaders has long been dead and you won't ever touch me again."

His eyes widened and he laughed. "Your soul has the icy clarity and incorruptible nature of the jewel covering you wear. I wonder what kind of woman you were on Aquama before you were installed in your mantle. You must understand, it is my nature to give expression to my desires. But you shall see. You will become more receptive to my attention after we've quit this tempestuous planet for the long silence of space travel. Until then, I shall have to test the depth of your vow of obedience to your commander. You must help me," he said, "you must help me destroy Vasthi and the Galactic Druid."

196

CHAPTER 22—Taxila Ambush

It was late afternoon and the closing ceremonies of the convention at the sports stadium were winding down. Vasthi was ecstatic; all 5000 slags had been selected and initiated into her service. She glanced up from her podium in the center of the field and looked out at the sea of faces swimming before her in the stands as the orchestral band played the Grand Canyon Suite. She turned to look at Josiah, seated behind her on the platform.

"It's done," she said. "It's done, and now we're ready to make great changes in the world." Her eyes glazed. "There has never been so many intellectually charged human beings in one place on earth as there is today, not ever."

Josiah looked out at the milling crowd standing and beginning to leave the stands. "Maybe you're right." He leaned forward, elbows on knees, hands clasped. "But where is our nemesis? Why hasn't he made any more attempts to disrupt it all?"

"I'm not so much worried about him anymore," Vasthi said. "Now he has to deal not only with me but with a legion of my followers. Perhaps that metallic beast fell into the Sacramento River and drowned."

"I doubt we'd have such luck," Josiah said, rising from his chair. "With a watertight beryllium sheath housing his organic being he might even float."

Vasthi stood and joined him in stepping down from the platform. "Put him out of mind. If it's our destiny to face him again why then so we shall, but for now we've beaten him."

"What's next?" he said, holding her hand and starting across the field.

"I had the political staff of the Foundation arrange meetings last night with cells of slags occupying key government and military positions around the world. Our analysis indicates two cells are already capable of engineering coups and gaining ruling power, in Indonesia and Pakistan. I plan to meet with the Pakistani cell and guide the coup development there. I'd like you to accompany me."

The wind blew strongly as they walked to the sideline. Two bodyguards followed close behind. "Maybe I'll just drop out of sight for a few weeks while you're on this excursion," Josiah said. "Go down to that little place I have in Quecha and be alone while I think about things."

The glow of enthusiasm vanished from her face and she stopped and bit at her lip. "I used to think I needed no one," she said. "Not anyone in this world. Oh, I suppose I've relied on people here and there, but not really needing them. You're different; it frightens me to admit it to myself but I need you." She bit at her lip and squeezed her eyes tighter. "Not for any special ability or powers that you may or may not have, but because I love you. You've become a part of me, who I am, my spirit. I could no more go on without you than I could stop being me. Perplexing discovery, isn't it?" She laughed without much pleasure and they continued walking. "I know my visions and goals disturb you," she said, "and perhaps you wish you could focus only on defeating Drost. Well, you may not be aware of it yet, but I've become a part of you, too. Perhaps the scale of it is different, but you won't forget me easily."

"You're absolutely right about that," he said.

"Give me a little more time with you, Josiah, to see whether I, too, can think things through more clearly, whether this world mission of mine is madness or whether it is the only possible life for me. I know you want me to veer from this course but stay with me a while longer. Come with me on my journey to Pakistan. Remember, you still have your mission to destroy Drost, and you won't be able to rest until it's done. We're alike in that, only your mission is given by some outside force while mine drives me from within."

"That's about right. I know I'll never have any peace until either Drost or I go to the grave, and I'm afraid I'd be destroyed by some grotesque, grand mal seizure if I tried to sidestep my mission. I'll go with you to Pakistan. Makes sense, too—wherever you go, Drost is sure to follow."

She stopped walking and put her arms around him. Josiah stroked her hair as the security guards opened the doors of the waiting limousine.

The message was delivered to them a week later when Vasthi and Josiah were in Pakistan. She read it aloud to him:

"The Night of the Macnessa is still young. The contest is yet to be decided between us and before the Dineen shall inherit the earth. Go at once to attend the ruins at Taxila."

She repeated the last sentence and walked to the wall to stare at a map.

Josiah came to stand beside her. "I get the shivers when I remember the Macnessa," he said. "Where is Taxila?"

199

"Here, on the road between Rawalpindi and Peshawar, along the plains close to the Himalayas. A curious place to choose," she said.

"Is it a town—what's there?"

"Archeological excavations. Quite a few civilizations rose and fell there—Persians, Greeks; Alexander himself was there. It met its final violent end from the White Huns of Central Asia."

"Eerie. It may have been specially chosen for another violent ending," Josiah said. "What could he be up to?"

"He's such a satanic genius," Vasthi said. "He has an awesome intellect and seems adept at manipulation of forces in the Universe that are beyond human experience or competence. Compared with him even the slags are like children. I've wondered, how old is Aquama? How old is Drost? We simply don't know. The one thing we do know is that Drost is vulnerable. A cohort of Indian peasants was able to destroy a Skatha many years ago and just by primitive force. You almost destroyed him, albeit with more sophisticated weaponry. The point is, he can be destroyed. We'll go to meet him at Taxila," she said.

At that moment, high above them, Drost and Eila sat in the Griffin viewing the hologram of the conspirators. Drost laughed as he tuned the control knob in the arm of his chair, producing an enlarged figure of Vasthi in the viewing arena.

"She's a beautiful creature, Eila, beautiful. A totally carnal animal but of extraordinary mental prowess for a human. I'd love to have bedded that one but it's probably too late for that now. I'm increasingly filled with a foreboding fear of remaining on this planet much longer. But before I leave, I'll strike a last mask of dread on their faces."

He stared at Vasthi's image as she spoke to the unseen Josiah telling him the Skatha can be destroyed, and a look of fright crossed Drost's face. Vasthi told of her plan to deploy military ground-to-air missile units around Taxila, to be used in the event the Griffin was spotted. Drost turned the volume up to listen better.

"We'll start a decoy motorcade on the highway toward Taxila at seven P.M. That ought to draw off the central government agents tracking our movements, as well as Drost if he plans to ambush us on the way to our meeting at Taxila. I'll instruct our people in the junta to deploy additional military units right away and to have a helicopter waiting for us outside this city at eight P.M."

Drost turned from the giant hologram of Vasthi, "As soon as they're in the air we'll attack," he said, and switched off the machine. Eila continued staring into the darkened viewing arena.

It was already night when Vasthi and Josiah drove onto a field next to an industrial plant outside Lahore. The giant rotor blade swirled and flattened the grass to the ground. The driver brought them close and they left the car and hurried crouched to the open helicopter door. Vasthi took the co-pilot's seat and Josiah sat behind. The pilot secured the cabin door.

"We are bound for Taxila, Memsahib?" the pilot asked

Vasthi in English.

"Yes, God willing," she said in Urdu, bringing a smile to the pilot's face at the familiar expression coming from a Westerner.

The helicopter lurched into the air and within minutes they flew high above the outskirts of the city heading north. Another few minutes and a myriad of white and colored lights winked up at them from the crowded bazaars and domiciles of the inner city. They continued on and took a slight, northwest bearing as the pilot cleared with a radio controller and referred to his flight map.

"Let's think about this a little more; why do you suppose he wants to meet with us at Taxila?" Josiah asked Vasthi in Spanish.

Vasthi glanced at the pilot and answered Josiah back in Spanish. "The setting must appeal to his sense of drama and he wants to negotiate something with us—or try to make another attempt on our lives."

"Let me see the telegram again," Josiah said. She reached into her pocket and handed it to him. He scanned it and read aloud one of the lines: "before the Dineen shall inherit the earth." That's the extinct prehistoric race he talked about on the Galapagos, but with a surviving consciousness and frozen within the rocks of Earth's surface. Did you know that fits the hypothesis of a Jesuit missionary geologist?"

She thought for a few seconds. "Yes, what was it Teilhard de Chardin conceived? Something like all mass in the Universe is endowed upon creation with some level of consciousness."

202

Josiah stared at her. "Even that you knew. Drost mentioned him, too; did he program that into your strands or is it from your own studies?"

"I no longer know where one ends and the other begins," she said.

"I see. Anyhow, I wrote to a nephew in the U.S. on the subject. He's a Jesuit and teaches geology at university."

"Did you tell him anything of the Skatha?" she said.

"He knows of my interest in Teilhard's books and philosophy and I've described my experience with the Skatha as a fiction I'm writing, to be synthesized with local Indian lore. One day when I feel the time is right I might suggest there could be elements of truth in my story and send him the manuscript for his comments."

"Trust me, Josiah, the time is not yet right for that. There is so much to be accomplished yet. Promise you'll talk about this again before you suggest to anyone that such things may be true."

He smiled and watched silently for a few moments. "All right. He knows of my seizures and probably would have doubts about his poor uncle's sanity anyhow. For now, I'll be keeping track of events in my journal. If I didn't write a little each day, I'd probably never believe it happened when I look back in years to come." He thought a moment. "If I have years to come."

"Be confident we have our best years ahead of us," she said.

Josiah started to speak when he saw something outside

the helicopter. A fluorescent blue glow lit up the sky around them and the familiar throbbing hum was heard above the stuttering engine of the helicopter. The blue light intensified, and they looked up through the plastic bubble cockpit to see the Griffin descending over them. Vasthi shouted an order to the pilot to yield the controls to her. A hatchway slid open in the floor of the craft above them. Vasthi veered the helicopter sharply to the side and shot up in altitude, rising above the Griffin.

"The assault rifle on the bulkhead—grab it and put a few rounds into their windows when I come about," she shouted to Josiah.

He grabbed for the rifle as she banked sharply and began a pass in front of the Griffin. Josiah slid open the cabin door and blasted a volley of shots into the Griffin.

"No use," he shouted. "The rounds are bouncing off the windows. Let's get out of here."

Vasthi plummeted down a thousand feet and veered to the left.

"Here he comes," Josiah shouted as he looked behind.

Vasthi dove another thousand feet, veered right, and dove again. Josiah's prothesis leg buckled and he fell when she pulled out of the dive. She skimmed over a rough, heavily eroded floodplain and along a river channel. Suddenly, she dropped the remaining one hundred feet and they bumped jarringly onto a flat, gravel bank. The helicopter swung around a few degrees while Vasthi unbuckled and leaped out of her seat.

"Hurry, we've got to make it into the brush," she shouted,

and she and Josiah jumped to the ground. They had their heat sink guns out, and as soon as the pilot leaped down they headed for the brush outlined by the helicopter landing lights.

Seconds later the blue glow enveloped the area. The throb of the Griffin pulsed as Josiah stumbled clumsily and lifted his heat sink gun toward the Griffin. A vaporous cloud streamed out from the underside of the Griffin and settled over them.

CHAPTER 23—Repository

Josiah awoke with a ringing in his ears and a bittersweet taste in his mouth. He pressed a hand over his eyes to ease the throbbing and sat up. A voice beside him moaned and he groped a hand over the curled mass of Vasthi's hair and touched her face. She moaned again and he dropped his hand from his eyes. The throbbing pain faded to a lesser pulse somewhere at the back of his head.

"Are you all right?" he said, his speech slurring.

She half-raised, winced, and lay back down on the cold rock surface. "Are we dead?"

"I don't think so. We're somewhere underground but I don't see any of the fires of hell." He got to his feet and looked around the dimly lit rock chamber.

"That's only because of our modest sins," Vasthi said. "We must be near one of the upper levels."

"You're right, it's Hell. Sit up and meet the Beelzebub; he looks just like I thought he might," Josiah said, a tired resignation in his voice.

Vasthi struggled to sit up, rubbing at her eyes until she could focus on the figure looming above her. "Drost," she said, forming his name in the sharp breath she exhaled.

"Yes, Drost, your master, whom you would spurn with your ill-advised self-pride and trenchant free will." He stood with hands on hips and shook his head. "Had you been pleased to consort with me, I could have laid the world at your feet. Instead, you would have liked to crush my head beneath those lovely feet. Enough, it is my Geise never to destroy a female of any order. I shall leave that to the Dineen whom we will now awaken from their long entombment. Let me tell you of—"

"Yes, yes, your Dineen tale," Vasthi said, rising to her feet. "Why would you think those distant cousins of your primitive, fulsome Macnessa would be a threat to the combined military might of today's nations?" She stood with hands on hips, facing him squarely.

Drost grew angry and his deep-set eyes glowered. "You are ignorant of the vast conquests made by this fierce and powerful race. Your own planet was once the whole of all the planets from Mercury to Saturn. The Dineen were but one of the races on that giant body, but they managed to subdue all the other inferior races. War and conquest were in their blood and if the Corso Cataclysm had not exploded, reordering your Galaxy into a sun and planets and absorbing the Dineen into the rocky wastes of the eruption, they would by now have ventured deep into space to conquer other worlds as well. Violence was their nature in their past life and will be their nature when revived."

"Nature has a way of cleansing itself of malignant mutations," Josiah said. "Maybe there'll never be a time they can return."

"Nature is an eternal cycle, Josiah, malignancies and corrections, each have their day and repeat over and over, each time evolving into some semblance of what has already been, but nothing is ever completely lost. The Dineen are closer to genetic reawakening today than any of the other races lying dormant in the Earth's crust and I have the means of hastening their awakening," Drost said, waving to a small cluster of equipment in the chamber.

Josiah stared at the heat-sink gun holstered at Drost's side. "If I don't end your miserable existence, other Galactic Druids will take up my task," he said.

"All existence is a contest," Drost said, forcing a stiff smile. "You may be interested in how your present existence will end. Vasthi will probably go first. I'll explain—it's exquisite. Dineen sorcerers led the wars of conquest. The first female captive from an enemy tribe was sacrificed, and her death cries were imprisoned in magical rattles. The death rattles were secretly carried into enemy territory, and at the sorcerers' commands screams from the rattles covered the land until the spirit of the opposing army was broken. The sound of the captive's blood sacrifice went into the ethereal quality of those screams, Vasthi, but I shall not try to describe it. I leave it to you to experience at the hands of the Dineen sorcerers."

As Drost spoke to Vasthi, Josiah moved closer to him. He took a quick glance at Eila who watched him but made no movement, and he rushed at Drost. Josiah grabbed for the heat-sink gun but Drost caught him and threw him back against the rock wall. Josiah crumpled to the ground, groaning and holding his side, his prothesis projected out awkwardly. Vasthi shouted and rushed at Drost but she was caught from behind. She struggled, shouting and kicking, but was pulled back. She twisted her head and stared into Eila's eyes. Eila released her and Vasthi turned to face her.

"You," she said, her voice a rushing hiss. "I'm not shocked that you'd join Drost to destroy me, but Josiah?"

"I've had to follow my commander's orders," Eila said, in a thick, hesitant voice.

"You'd do nothing to save Josiah, you Skatha witch?" Vasthi shouted, shoulders bunched, and fists clenched. "You've drugged yourself into a stupor so that you could do this, haven't you?"

Vasthi flew at Eila, striking fists at her head and tearing at her hair. Josiah seized the distraction to hurl himself again at Drost. The struggle was over quickly as the Skatha held and subdued them. Vasthi's anger and helplessness were too much for her and she burst into tears. Drost picked up a coil of rope, forced Josiah against a wall, and trussed his hands behind his back.

"That should keep you a bit more manageable until we are ready to part company, Druid." He tossed the remainder of the coil to Eila, and in a few minutes she had Vasthi bound. Vasthi continued to struggle as she tried to choke off her sobs of rage and frustration. Josiah leaned against the rock wall and glared at Drost. Once, his eyes met Eila's and a terrible disappointment clouded his face. She stared back, squeezed her eyes shut, and turned away.

"Keep a watch over them while I set up," Drost said, and he hurried to the stack of equipment leaning against a wall.

Josiah looked about him. Some sort of excavated rock chamber, maybe about thirty feet high. A smaller, horseshoe-shaped tunnel entered the chamber at one side, near the equipment, and another one exited at the opposite wall. He stepped forward until he could see down the length of the tunnel. Lights hung from the tunnel roof and showed side openings all along its length.

Drost stopped sorting through his equipment and spoke to Josiah. "All those side tunnels hold canisters of spent nuclear rods from your power plants," Drost said. "The entire available space in this nuclear waste repository has been filled to capacity and is waiting to be sealed off from the surface in six months from now."

Drost removed the screen of a sheet metal ventilation duct running along the top of the tunnel and installed his isotope accelerator inside the duct. He wired a power amplifier onto the ventilation fan motor circuit. When he switched on the power, a pencil-thin beam of blue laser light from the isotope accelerator projected inside the length of the ventilation duct. Drost hurried along the main tunnel and installed a beam-splitting prism in the duct at each branching point with a side tunnel.

As Drost worked, Eila kept guard over Vasthi and Josiah. She moved constantly about the tunnel chamber, walking aimlessly in an agitated manner.

"You once led me to believe you might help me to destroy him," Josiah said as she passed by him.

She stopped and stared at the ground. "My oaths of loyalty, not only to him but to our leaders, have weighed heavily on me," she said. "I wish I'd drowned in the sea after Vasthi shot me. It was my ill fortune to have Drost find and rescue me and bring me back to health."

"I've believed you were just as evil as Drost," Vasthi said. "You could show Josiah how wrong I was by helping us now."

"You can do it," Josiah said. "You're just at a low point.

Any vows you took back then didn't anticipate how corrupted Drost would become. This is now, and a lot of terrible things have happened since then. Just get these ropes off us and give me that gun. I'll take care of Drost."

Eila tore at her hair, clapped her hands over her ears, and walked across the chamber away from them, shoulders shaking.

After Drost had finished his preparations in the tunnel, he hurried back to the rock chamber. "There shouldn't be anyone coming down here until the sealing operations start," he said. "If my calculations are right it won't take much time at all for the Dineen's resurrection, and we'll be monitoring events from the Griffin just in case."

He hurried past Josiah to get the remaining amino gas synthesizer equipment. He placed the injection nozzle from the synthesizer into the main ventilation duct just downstream of the fan. "I couldn't have asked for a better delivery system than what was already here." He straightened and stepped back to survey his handiwork. "Now, if my calculations of existing bio-energy levels in the Dineen rock are correct, the isotope accelerator will trigger enough completion energy from the radioactive waste to begin the process. The Dineen should reach a threshold of life in about two weeks. After that, our amino gas isotopes will provide the final catalyst for exploding their consciousness into renewed, glorious, organic life."

"And what if your calculations are wrong?"

Drost gave Josiah a pitiful look, "As soon as we witness the epic spectacle of their arousal, we'll return to Tupa Inca and take leave of this accursed planet in the Epoch-3."

"How many Dineen will there be?" Vasthi said, staring at the walls and roof as if to discern their outlines. An edge of despair touched her voice.

Drost smiled and rubbed his chin, "Let's say the isotope accelerator generates optimum chain reactions with the nuclear waste energy. I estimate the self-perpetuating reaction products could irrigate two square miles of these waste tunnels, and the geologic maps show the rock flow entombing our Dineen friends is about two hundred feet thick. I think we can count on releasing about two to three million Dineen, allowing for some low-consciousness or unresponsive waste rock."

Vasthi drew a breath at the mention of such a staggering number. Josiah took another look at the walls, envisioning an ever-multiplying horde of Dineen bursting into the opening. He shook his head and tried to refocus his thoughts on their immediate situation.

"Bring us the ceremonial robes," Drost said to Eila. She picked up a carton near the tunnel entrance and carried it to him. "I've researched the annals stored on our on-board computer bank," Drost said. "This costume is representative of ceremonial dress prescribed by Dineen sorcerers for the sacrifice of any high-ranking woman captured from an enemy. Magical powers were attached to the spirits of certain beasts and birds of their world and they invoked that magic by offering human sacrifice to the animals."

"Untie her," he said to Eila as he unpacked the box. Eila hesitated and moved to undo Vasthi's bonds. The rope fell away from Vasthi's wrists and she massaged them to bring back circulation.

"Strip her of what she wears, and we'll clothe her for the ritual," Drost said.

Eila reached to undo her blouse and Vasthi seized and held her wrist.

Josiah made an awkward start toward them but Drost's voice boomed, "Be reasonable, Vasthi. If you resist our ceremonies I shall slay the Druid now instead of allowing him to await the Dineen in your company."

Drost cocked the lever on his heat-sink gun and aimed it at Josiah. Vasthi grimaced and let her hand fall from Eila's wrist. Eila removed Vasthi's apparel until she was stripped to the waist. She paused as she stood before the beautiful, olive-hued torso of the defiant woman, then tore angrily at the rest of Vasthi's clothes until she'd stripped her completely.

Vasthi's skin glistened with perspiration in the humidity of the underground chamber. She had a wild and anxious look on her face, though she stood straight and poised before Drost. His hands trembled holding the Snowy Owl headdress and he stared at her. He stepped forward and lifted it above her head. Eila flattened Vasthi's curls as Drost seated her headdress. A black beak projected from the billowing white plumage and rested on the bridge of Vasthi's nose, and the owl's eye cavities framed her own wide, darting eyes.

"You're an appropriate vessel for the guile and magic powers the Dineen ascribed to their ancient precursor of the Snowy Owl," he said, and he stepped back to observe her. He reached into the box and lifted out another garment, shook it out with a flourish to reveal a long, brown-flecked, white feather cloak, and swept it about her shoulders,

214

clasping it at the throat. He let his hand rest on her shoulder. "Your cloak is made from the plumage of the most royal of birds, a gyrfalcon, whose ancestor the Dineen venerated for its courage and savagery in the hunt. If they could know you as I have, they might have suspected the gyrfalcon was no match for your own courage." He moved to reach an arm around her waist but Vasthi stepped back. Drost betrayed his chagrin with a scowl and he turned to lift another article from the box—a long, white-furred pelt with an attached bear claw. He tossed it to Eila and she wrapped the pelt around Vasthi's waist, leaving the tasseled claw dangling to her thigh.

"A polar bear, its ancestor noted then as now for a singular instinct to stalk man, as well as for a bloodlust in devouring its prey," Drost said.

He stared at the exotically garbed, sensually charged woman before him and passed a hand inside his shirt to massage his articulated, metallic surface. He glanced around at the others.

"Don't even think such a thing," Eila said.

Drost's hands shook and his vocal cords fibrillated to produce high-pitched sounds in his throat. He seized Vasthi by her wrist and pulled her to him, lifting her cape to uncover a shoulder, lavishing his tongue over her craving some sensual contact, and plunged his head to her breasts. Vasthi screamed and struggled in his iron grip.

Eila cut Josiah free of his bonds.

He staggered up and at Drost, striking him with a body block and toppling him to the rock floor. Straddling Drost and seizing his head, Josiah struck it repeatedly against the rock. Drost reached up and grabbed Josiah by his collar, twisting it to throttle him. Josiah was unable to break the overpowering leverage of Drost's arm and made a desperate grab at the heat-sink gun holstered at Drost's side. He got the gun only to have it spin from his grasp as Drost slammed him down on the rock floor. The gun skidded away and Vasthi dashed for it. Drost raged and struck at Josiah as he rolled away to escape the bruising blows. Drost pursued him on his knees striking at him, till he saw Vasthi holding the heat-sink gun.

"No," Drost screamed. "Eila, kill her, kill her."

Eila had her own heat-sink gun trained on Vasthi, steadying her shaking aim with both hands. In the seconds that Drost watched Vasthi arm the heat-sink gun at full power and raise it, he saw Eila close her eyes and lower her own weapon.

"Traitor," he shrieked at Eila as he rose and lunged at Vasthi with blurring speed. He closed with her and deflected the gun as she fired a short burst. She struggled to twist free of his grasp but he closed his powerful arms about her shoulders. He laughed but choked it off when he looked down to see she still had the gun flattened against his chest. She slid her arm upward and the gun muzzle rose toward his chin. His terror of death overwhelmed the terror of breaking his sacred Geise. He sought Vasthi's lips and summoned his maximum surge of fire-tonguing power beyond any level needed for sheath transfer. Desperately Vasthi called on her own feeble, slagging charge. Electrical shock waves vibrated in the air and an intense blue glow enveloped the struggling figures. An acrid burning smell filled the chamber and drifted about. Josiah struggled to his feet, saw what happened, and covered his eyes.

216

Drost stared at the ashes of Vasthi on his arms and torso. A low, sobbing gurgle rose in his throat culminating in an insane scream as he realized what he'd done. He'd destroyed her at his own hands—committed the ultimate sin against his Geise. He stumbled away, falling to his knees and rising again, shielding his eyes from the terrible demons pursuing him in his mind. Bellowing a fear-crazed anguish, he ran from the chamber.

Eila was also shaken. She looked at the scattering of ashes and plumage on the floor, covered her eyes for a moment, and slowly walked over to put a hand on Josiah's shoulder as he wept.

CHAPTER 24—Odyssey

The night was pitch-black when Eila and Josiah stepped from the elevator at the surface of the repository shaft. Josiah was still dazed.

"So terrible…so awful to live through. Why couldn't I have done something more? She had such crazy dreams but she was so alive. So alive. And now…where is she? Where are you, Vasthi?"

Eila looked away for a moment. "She was a remarkable woman but we've got to focus on our own situation—Drost is still out there. What do we do now?"

Josiah let out a deep breath and shook his head, trying to surface from his thoughts. "Do you have both guns?" he said, his throat sore where Drost's vise-like grip had held him.

"Yes, I picked Drost's up from her—her ashes." She took a gun from her rucksack and handed it to him.

Josiah grimaced and scanned the area, passing over the shades of grays and blacks marking the service buildings and shops. "Drost might have calmed down and waited for us to come up," he said. "More than ever I want to destroy him now. I'm wondering where you might stand with that? It's been hard to read your actions up to now."

"Is it? Twice on your behalf I've broken vows made to Drost and our leaders when I volunteered for this space mission."

Josiah looked away to the shrubs nearby rustling in the wind and back to her. It was hard to make out her expression in the dim moonlight. The soft luster of her hair, a filmy play of light sweeping the high cheekbones.

"Let's keep moving," he said, putting a hand to her shoulder and urging her away from the buildings and toward a perimeter of brush. "By the way, what were those vows?"

"Absolute loyalty to my mission commander, Drost, assuming the role of paramate, to him, and observing chastity for the duration of the exploratory mission.

They reached the scattered stands of coyote brush and creosote shrubs and paused. Josiah inspected the arming mechanism of his gun.

"I know your disloyalty to that madman saved my life more than once," he said, "back at the park tent, and below in the repository. I'm glad you were able to see the circumstances of your vow might have changed. Circumstances have changed for me, too. Before, I'd just been trying to follow Akla's orders to destroy the Beryllium Eaters. Well, now it's my own vow—to destroy Drost. You can be sure I'd never do anything to harm you."

"That's all—that's all there is to it?"

"There's always been more than that between us, but I haven't let myself think about it. Tell me about your role of paramate and vow of chastity."

"That," she said, "well," and she paused for a moment. "I told you of conditions on Aquama that led us to become bio-metallic creatures, in order to survive our harsh, new environment. At that time, all Skatha procreation was

220

forbidden, until we could find a new world more hospitable to the true, genetic nature of our race—a nature you know to be much like your own."

"You could have had children, even after the—the sheathing?"

"Yes, but on Aquama they would have to have been extraordinarily sheltered until they were grown and sheathed themselves. It's one of the many things that drove us to search for another home. Most of the other inhabited planets of our universe bred strange, alien races living under conditions that made even the declining Aquama world seem preferable, so our leaders made a decision to probe for other, more habitable worlds for us, deeper into space than we'd ever ventured before. They ordered five missions to be made ready, each recruited from one of the five provinces of Aquama. The male commander of each ship was a Skatha warrior of high rank, and his female consort was chosen from a noble family, descended from the Lordly Ones who'd first inhabited Aquama."

"Did you know Drost before your mission?"

"No, I was from a mountainous region and he was from a distant, desert region." She grew silent, as if thinking about long ago.

"You were also saying—about chastity, and your vow?"

She looked up, startled. "Yes, well the missions were expected to be of long duration, and our leaders, in their wisdom, temporarily pledged the woman paramate and her vow of chastity to the ship commander. This was to safeguard against contaminating the ancient Skatha race with the seed of any alien races contacted during the exploration."

"So they put a woman aboard to satisfy the man's needs?"

"That wasn't the reason," Eila said. "Exploitation was thought to be a matter of low probability because a male's tactile senses were severely limited. It was only after we arrived here that Drost discovered how to overcome his sensual limitation at the expense of humans. The reason a woman member needed to be sent on an expedition was in fulfillment of certain passages in the sacred books of the Skatha foretelling our crisis and forced emigration from Aquama. The woman's role is to help choose the new world to be colonized by our people and only the women were to be permitted to vote on this matter when the missions returned to Aquama."

"But you've been away for a very long time. Maybe the other expeditions have already gone back and voted?"

"Yes, it's possible," she said, a deep weariness dulling her voice. "Perhaps I should have destroyed Drost myself when he refused to go back all those times I begged him in the past. We were expected to return long ago and vote on the question of Skatha colonization of Earth."

"Invade Earth?" He shook his head, stunned.

"Why not? It's a wondrous and inviting place."

Josiah was learning to read the emotions in her voice—a hint of irony now. At least Aquama hadn't had any report on Earth. Maybe they'd already voted and were on their way to another colony. "We're losing time," he said. "Drost is out

222

here somewhere. We need to separate a little and try and catch him off guard, but I'm wondering whether you're ready for this?"

"I've tried to be faithful to our mission but he's made a shambles of it, and now that he's broken his Geise I don't know what else he'll do. If it falls to me to end his transgression, I think I can do it now. We should start out for the Griffin. If he can regain his senses after what's happened, that's where he'll go." She took out her command module, activated the locator function, and noted the landmarks in the direction the module indicated. "Keep yourself online with the dog star in Sirius, there, the brightest one. We can stay separated by about fifty meters as we walk. The Griffin is only about a kilometer away."

They advanced through the brushy terrain, moving away from the repository complex. As he walked, Josiah thought of how he'd never been able to fully commit himself to Vasthi, always evasive, never fully accepting her unbridled passion to prevail over forces of evil. And yet, he'd felt deeply about her. He might have reached some acceptable accommodation with her but he would never know that for sure now. All of a sudden, this strange woman from another planet seems to have become the rational trajectory for his life purpose.

He stopped frequently as he went, listening over the soughing wind. He hadn't gone far before a loud rustle of leaves and snapping twigs erupted close by. His stomach tightened and he strained to see if it was Drost rushing at him from out of the night. More crashing through the brush and getting closer. He dropped to the ground on his good leg and steadied the heat-sink gun on the prothesis with both hands. The creature erupted from the brush and charged.

Frantic, he realized he hadn't armed the gun yet and smacked the lever back to full power as he felt the ground shaking. In the instant before activating, the dark form veered away to his left across his line of sight. It was a long time before he could lower the gun in his rigidly locked arms and his jaw trembled at the sight of the wild boar crashing through the brush.

Josiah continued on his way, keeping the dog star aligned with a distant peak. The cold empty feeling in his stomach almost matched the chill in the air. In empty stretches of ground the wind blew sharp, pinpricks of sand that bit into his face. Once, he caught sight of Eila in the distance, but his eyes stung in the gritty wind and then she was gone. Passing into thicker brush, thorns scraped at his clothing. He'd looked ahead at a dusky mound for more than a hundred yards and as he approached closer the dim moonlight revealed the camouflaged surface of the Griffin.

Josiah felt for the setting of the power lever on the gun. Drost had to be in the craft. He crouched and moved forward, stopping when he saw a figure move from the brush to behind the craft. It was Eila. He continued around the craft and met her.

"Any sign of him?" he said.

"None."

"He's got to be inside."

"No, I don't think so. I've got the command module to enter the Griffin. I had a feeling things wouldn't go well tonight and I didn't leave the module in its usual hiding place when we left. If he's around here, he's been waiting for us."

Josiah turned and scanned the perimeter of brush. The Griffin had set down in a large, bare patch of ground. "Move over next to the hatch and open it," he said. "I'll watch for any movement out of the brush."

Eila activated the module and the hatchway slid open. They waited, weapons drawn, scanning the open field. Nothing moved.

Eila said, "He was so crazed with fear after breaking his Geise that he may not have recovered yet."

"You're probably right or he would have been on us by now."

"Let's leave before the sun rises," Eila said.

"What's he likely to do when he comes to his senses?"

"He might go to a cabin he had somewhere near here while he investigated the rock formations and the repository. After he gets over his catastrophe, he'll probably want to return to Tupa Inca."

"Okay, we'll go back there and wait for him. But first, I want to return to the repository. I need to spend a few minutes with Vasthi and Drost's equipment needs to be put out of commission."

Eila touched his arm and her eyes had a troubled look. "Yes, I understand. It all happened so quickly; I don't know if I could have saved her. I didn't know what I was doing down there."

"I should be back in an hour, at most," he said.

Later, sitting with legs drawn up, and back propped against the wall in the mining chamber, he looked vacantly about. He whispered several times to himself and rested his head on his arms. He sat for a long time, lifting his head now and then to lean back against the wall, murmured disjointed words—could have, should have—till he thrust his legs out flat and dropped his arms to his side. He stayed with head bowed for a while, then rose and went to the isotope accelerator. Lifting open a panel, he inspected the wiring. Opening a pocketknife, he listened to a barely audible hum of the controls and began cutting circuits. The humming ceased. He replaced the panel and turned his attention to the gas synthesizer. In a few minutes he'd disabled that, too.

He waved at the wall of rock around him. "Sleep well, Dineen. May you never rise again on this planet."

Eila was seated at the controls when he got back to the Griffin. She watched him as he stepped through the cabin door and came over and dropped into the chair beside her. He stared at the computer monitor screen in front of him and saw it was tuned to the view inside the mining chamber where he'd just left.

"I worried that Drost might have seen you and followed you underground," she said. "I've scanned the area dozens of times since you left but saw no sign of him at the surface or underground."

"Right, let's get going to Tupa Inca."

She strapped in and motioned for him to do the same. After punching in the flight commands and setting the controls she looked over at him. He nodded and she flicked a switch. The engine throbbed momentarily and settled into

226

a barely audible hum. Watching through the forward hatch windows, Josiah saw the encircling brush awash in the blue glow given off by the craft. The Griffin lifted abruptly and Josiah's senses reeled. Another few seconds and they accelerated laterally. A few moments later he turned to her, the color still drained from his face.

"Not exactly your standard, commercial airliner," he said. "Hope the landing is a bit smoother."

"She smiled. "Sorry, I've gotten into the habit of thinking of you so often that I forget you're human and take you for another Skatha."

"I never know what to make of you," he said.

"I'm Skatha, just Skatha," she said, busying herself reading gages.

Josiah watched the swirling starlight through the hatch windows, mulling over the exotic, feminine creature beside him. She'd always aroused in him what he could only admit as a bizarre desire, an improbable fantasy.

She turned to him, "Have you never wanted me in the manner of a man for a woman of your race?" she said.

He lowered his hand from his chin and cleared his throat. "I wouldn't say I hadn't thought about it. Mostly, though, I'd only thought of Vasthi once she entered my life."

Eila nodded and leaned back into her flight chair. "Yes, I'd been painfully aware that you'd moved away from me after the magical, initial bond that seemed to form between us. For the first time in many years I consulted the Skatha oracles but received only an incomplete answer. Vasthi's

227

early return to the inanimate consciousness realm was foretold and also that the bond between you and I might grow stronger."

Josiah got up from his chair and paced the command deck. "Did your oracle have anything to say about the outcome of my mission to destroy Drost?"

"Nothing of that."

He leaned against a port window and watched the lights of cities swirl beneath them. "Do you have a drink on board?"

"I'll bring something," she said, and left the command deck for a lower level. She returned with a tray carrying two bottles of wine and glasses. Josiah followed her past the navigation consoles to an observation deck facing onto a wide, two-meter high window rising from floor level. She set the tray on a low table and opened a panel beneath to take out a soft, alpaca rug and cushions. She pressed a console button to retract two observation chairs into the floor and placed the rug and cushions in the empty space before the window.

"Sit here with me," she said. "We're traveling at a low velocity to conserve the small amount of beryllium fuel we have left but that allows us to enjoy the wonderful panorama of Earth's face." She arranged the wine and glasses to one side and stretched herself out on the rug to lay her head on a cushion and watch through the window. "I often took excursions from Tupa Inca in the early years after we first arrived here, to fly over your planet and thrill to the beautiful forms and shades of color that cover its surface."

He took the glass she offered and lay down beside her to

watch out the window. Blocks and ribbons of lights ran pell-mell over the dark ground surface below. A shimmering surface of moonlit sea edged into view on one side as they streaked south. The first glass of Argentine Malbec went down smoothly and he watched as she poured another. She lifted her glass, toasting him in words he couldn't understand. He stared into the pale, icey blue irises of her eyes, and from the pulsar energy there, down to the high cheek planes tapering quickly to the small chin, all framed within curtains of silvery hair. A full, generous mouth, verging on a hesitant smile. He searched the complexion of her face, pale, aquamarine, a smooth symmetry of countless micro-planes, flowing over rounded contours softening the macro-planes of light.

Josiah reached out to touch her face, remembering the first time in Kepo's cabin, shivering again at the silk-like smoothness of the jewel surface. His fingers moved over her face to her lips. The luster of moonlight through the window highlighted the fine-grained surface of her lips where her inner organic being penetrated so close to the beryllium mantle.

He held her chin and lowered his face, brushing his lips over hers, and brought his mouth hard onto hers. The sound of both their voices grew muffled and they lay back onto the rug. He pressed his tongue past her lips and found the startling warmth and dizzying sensation of her tongue. They moved erratically at first, drawing back from time to time, each to study the face of this somehow kindred creature, so exotically different, so much the same.

He sat up and began removing his shirt, paused as he took off a shoe, and wondered what sort of bizarre experience could unfold. He shrugged his shoulders and took off the prothesis, too. He was letting this happen so soon after Vasthi, but in her Machiavellian way she'd have approved. She cared little for Eila, but would probably advise him to get Eila's help against Drost using whatever strategy worked. He shook his head. She might have slipped him one of those slagging capsules after all. By the time he'd turned back to Eila, mind clouded over, uncertain of anything, she'd removed her clothes. The jeweled luster and supple molding of her body, each tiny facet, each floating free of the other, was as delicate and beautiful as her face, and her hair lay cascaded around her like silver gossamer.

They lay entwined for a long time afterward. When he raised his head to look out the window, only a few, far-off mantles of light showed on the ground. Mountains lay below, huge shifting expanses of gray whites and charcoal blacks, hinting already of dawn.

"Maybe we ought to check our position. Might have overshot by now," he said.

She murmured in sleepy tones, "I programmed us to circle above Tupa Inca when we arrived. Would you have had us interrupted just to land?"

He shook his head. So astonishing. Was it all a matter of sensation and pheromones flooding the brain or was there sometimes a higher, spiritual communion? He leaned down to kiss her, and stared out again at the gradual lighting of the snow-capped, high peaks of the Andes. A beautiful country. He thought of his small ranch near the foot of those majestic mountains. His face grew more somber as he thought, there was still the problem of Drost.

CHAPTER 25—The Crucible

The first two days back at Tupa Inca were times of growing attachment between Josiah and Eila, though Vasthi's memory continued to hover in Josiah's mind. She still retained a spiritual presence, intent on seeing him through the coming encounter with Drost.

On the third day, as he and Eila made their rounds of the underground facilities, Josiah noticed the absence of any Indian workers.

"They're all gone," he said. "Something's wrong."

"Yes, it seems ominous," Eila said. "They sometimes go off to visit their kin, but usually a core staff remains. Perhaps it's only that they've become aware of our unease, and they've stayed at their homes today."

"Maybe. I scanned all the surveillance and detection systems this morning," he said. "Nothing. Maybe we need to go outside, take a short flight in the Griffin and survey things from above?"

"We could do that."

"But first, I'd like to get a closer look at the Epoch-3," he said. "The surveillance camera was a little murky for that location and I couldn't make things out too well."

"Yes, I've been meaning to take you there to see it up close. We'll use the elevator up to the holding bay."

They walked to the central hub of the tunnel system,

entered the elevator, and rose seventy meters before coming to a halt. The door opened onto a lighted, stone-lined tunnel. A cool, dry air circulated through the tunnel and lifted Eila's hair as they left the elevator. They strode toward an end portal about fifty meters distant and passed an intersecting tunnel along the way.

"Where does that one lead?" Josiah said.

"To a stairway down to the metallurgical plant."

They reached the end portal of the tunnel and stepped into a large, dimly lit vault. Eila flicked a switch for additional overhead lighting and the interstellar Epoch-3 came out of the shadows. About seventy-five meters long and five meters in diameter, the ship had a flattened, elliptical nose and a bulbar midship section that housed a gravity simulator to ease physiological stress on long flights. A streamlined pod swept down from the nose and opened aft into a wide bay for in-flight docking and launching of the Griffin. A tail section ended in a cluster of huge thrust jets.

Josiah whistled softly as he scanned the awesome craft that had spanned the universe between the world of the Skatha and this world. "Is it ready to go?"

"Yes," she said. "Drost and I went through a complete check of systems immediately after it was fueled last week." She paused, unable to form her next words.

"What is it?" Josiah said.

"Come with me to Aquama," she said.

He was stunned. "Aquama? Your scientists would have to convert me into another bio-metallic being."

"Your words are crueler than you can imagine. I don't want to leave you, but I'm afraid. As I am, I'm perhaps too strange for you to fathom, much less to completely love. Yet, within I'm the same being as you. I can be as good for you as any woman on Earth," she said. She put her arms around him and held him tightly.

The launch bay was suddenly plunged into darkness. "The lights—what happened?" Josiah shouted. A stunning blow sent him spinning to the floor and Eila cried out. An iron grip fixed around Josiah's ankle and his brain registered the hulking form of Drost dragging him closer. Josiah grabbed at his belt for the heat-sink gun--it was gone."

"Eila, it's him—shoot," he cried out.

A white beam of light hissed through the darkness and Josiah's leg was free. He scrambled to his feet as Eila stood beside him.

"I don't hear anything," she said.

"Did you paint him with that ray?"

"Yes, I think so, but it was so short."

"Come on, let's get moving," Josiah said. "He has my heat-sink gun."

They moved along the wall toward the entry and out into the passageway.

"We'll take the elevator up to the Griffin's bay and wait for him to come to us," she said.

They ran through the tunnel to the elevator. Inside, she

punched a control button—nothing happened. "He must have cut the elevator power," she said. "Quick, follow me to the stairway." They rushed out and paused to listen over the thrum of air within the tunnel.

"No sign of him," Josiah said. "Maybe you hit him with a lethal dose."

"He didn't go down. At best, he was only stunned and now he's armed, too—let's go," she said, and they hurried back along the tunnel.

A hulking figure entered the tunnel from the Epoch-3 vault at the far end. Josiah froze as the figure lumbered toward them.

"Quick, we'll take cover in the metallurgical plant and wait there," Eila said, pulling Josiah into the side tunnel and plunging down the stairway.

Inside the plant a fiery glow of molten metal in huge vats below them lit the room with an eerie light. They ran along the metal grate catwalk, looking for somewhere to take cover, as Drost leaped down onto the catwalk behind them. They reached a doorway.

"Jammed—I can't get it open," Josiah said, struggling with the sliding bolt. Eila spun about and crouched. Just as she raised her heat-sink gun, the lethal white ray of Drost's weapon hissed across the space and Eila pitched forward onto the catwalk. Her weapon dropped from her hand and fell into a bubbling vat below.

"Eila," Josiah shouted, and rushed to stop her from rolling off the edge of the catwalk. He crouched and grabbed around her waist as Drost came up.

"It was because of you I've come to this end, Space Druid," he said. "My Geise has been broken, my dreams of power are laid waste, and my Skatha paramate has betrayed me. I am weary of this existence."

Eila groaned and rubbed at the numbness in her shoulder, then sat upright. Drost watched as Josiah helped her to her feet.

"I'm glad my ray only stunned you, Eila," Drost said. "I want to embrace you one last time before the secrets of Tupa Inca are obliterated forever."

"Why—what have you done?" Eila said.

"Explosive gases are circulating through the ventilation systems while we speak. When the gases reach this room and the concentration becomes sufficiently strong, it will be ignited by the furnaces below. Or perhaps when the timer I've set for the Epoch-3 engines activates and it launches, unmanned, into space."

Josiah smelled the gas seeping into the room.

"You intend for us all to perish in the blast?" he said.

Drost smiled. "Certainly you will be blown to pieces my frail friend, but there might be a chance that Eila and I would survive and I couldn't allow that—not now." He put his arm about her waist. "She and I will leap together into the molten metal below."

Eila lifted a fist to her mouth and her eyes widened. She tried to scream but fainted and slipped from Drost's arm onto the catwalk. He stooped to get her and Josiah tackled him behind the knees. With a terrible cry, Drost pitched forward, tripped across Eila, and fell headlong into the vat below. He struggled to rise above the boiling surface of gangue on the molten metal, screaming as the searing heat penetrated his sheath. Josiah helped Eila to her feet and they stared as Drost began to sink until only a gangue-covered, claw-like hand stuck above the frothing surface. The surface rose in a mound, belched to release a burst of gas, and he was gone.

"Such a terrible demise, even for Drost," Eila said, and held her arm over her eyes.

"He was a genius that could have made a brilliant, mythical name for the Skatha," Josiah said. Instead, he left only a darkness. Let's get out of here; the gas smell is getting stronger."

"Yes, quick, follow me up this stairway." She shot back a deadbolt and threw open the door. They hurried from the metallurgical plant and groped their way up the dark stairwell. Josiah's throat burned and his head ached. The prothesis binding pained him and he climbed the stairs using both hands and dragging the hurt limb.

"Hurry, Josiah, hurry," Eila shouted back. "We've got to get to the Griffin."

They reached the top and hurried along another narrow passage to the next flight of stairs. Josiah fell and lay gasping before reaching the top. Eila, too, reeled as gas vapors swirled around them but she caught Josiah with one arm beneath his shoulders and dragged him up the remaining stairs.

236

CHAPTER 26—Shooting Stars

On the mountainside below Tupa Inca, Kepo stood outside his house and gasped when he looked up and saw the interstellar space craft lift up into the night sky, the brilliance of its thrust jets illuminating a fiery trail across the night sky. Seconds later, he toppled over as the ground shook and explosions above sent shock waves hammering through the air. Brilliant, flaring lights and multicolored streamers illuminated the sky above the mountaintop for several minutes, and soon all grew dark and quiet.

CHAPTER 27—Rancho Quecha

On a late fall afternoon in the foothills near Quecha, two men drove up to a small ranch. An Indian servant met them in the driveway and escorted the men along a garden walk to a covered porch surrounding the house. Josiah rose from a chair on the porch to receive the visitors.

"Josiah Dermot?" the taller, bearded man said. "We've come with greetings from your nephew, Terrill."

Josiah smiled and reached out a hand. "Welcome. Terrill wrote last month that I could expect visitors from the university," he said. "I hope you've had a pleasant trip of it, so far."

"Tiring, but we're glad to be here. I'm Father Hugh Clarke and this is Father Mark Brown—Terrill's associates in the anthropology department. We're just returning from our exploration into the remains of Tupa Inca. I'm afraid we weren't able to accomplish much on this trip—the site seems in such a state of disrepair and quite overgrown with vegetation. Terrill said you had some extensive knowledge of Inca history in the region and might be willing to discuss it with us. Would this be a convenient time to talk?"

Josiah stood silently with hands on hips for a few moments, a sparely built man, hair streaked with gray, a few lines etched at the corners of his eyes and near his mouth. He motioned a servant to bring chairs for the visitors.

"You'll hardly find me an authority on Inca history at Tupa Inca," he said, as they sat and were served coffee by a servant. "Years ago I worked on the hydroelectric powerhouse near there and I heard many stories about Tupa Inca from the local Indian people. Some stories may have had kernels of truth in them while others seemed quite bizarre."

"Yes, I heard from Terrill that you've collected some of those stories. Between Mark and I, we speak several Indian dialects of the Andes; however, we weren't able to get anyone to tell us much about Tupa Inca."

"It used to be that they'd discuss it with outsiders but in more recent years they've become wary of speaking about it," Josiah said.

"I understand one of the theories for the upheaval evident at the site was that it was struck by a meteor," Mark said. "Do you give any credence to that?"

"It's one of the stories told. Other, more fanciful tales tell of it being destroyed by the gods. I prefer the latter tale but that's me. Nonetheless, a government geologist did find fragments of unusual rock in a crater-like formation at the site. It contained rare isotopes of beryllium but it was unclear from the analyses whether it might have been from a meteor."

"Extraordinary and unfortunate," the men murmured.

They talked for almost two hours and Josiah told them of the local legend of the gods from another world who came to support the Inca in their wars of conquest, and of the fearful fire-tongue sacrifice to propitiate the warrior gods. He told them how elements of the same Inca mythology had permeated trappings of the modern Inca Foundation, the international environmental movement that had become popular and then disappeared some years before.

The professors recalled the Foundation and nodded.

The men switched to brandy as it became dusk and a light rain fell. Two figures on horseback approached across an open field. The men watched as the riders came up, dismounted, and handed over their horses to a servant. They came onto the lighted porch and the professors stood with Josiah to greet them. Both were dressed in oilskin ponchos over riding britches. One was a girl, perhaps fifteen or sixteen. She removed her wide leather sombrero and let fall a cascade of almost silver-like hair, striking, given her youth. Her blue eyes and rain-streaked fair complexion lent a radiance to her smile as she greeted Josiah and his guests.

"I think I'll turn in early, Dad," she said to Josiah. "Mother and I probably rode fifty miles today and I'm cold and soaked through from the last five miles in the rain."

Standing apart from the group, the tall woman still wore her sombrero low on her forehead and her silk riding scarf was wound about her lower face. Dramatically, the same silvery hair as the daughter flowed from beneath her scarf and down her back. She nodded at the guests and looked to Josiah.

"They're professors from the States," he said. "Interested in legends of Tupa Inca. Would you want to talk about any of the stories we've heard from the Indians?"

A few light notes of laughter, like muffled wind chimes and she reached for the door held open by her daughter. "I've lived with those stories for so long I'm fearful I might intrude some of my own fantasies into them. I'm sure you'll give more useful and objective narratives to our learned guests."